Souls UNITED

I love the first book and the second book was even better. It kept me turning the pages long into the night!

~ S
Goodreads reviewer

Souls United

SOUL WEAVER DUOLOGY BOOK TWO

CHANTELLE LAMBERT

Identifiers:
ISBN-13: 978-0-6488867-6-1 (paperback 5x8in)
ISBN-13: 978-1-7635490-0-5 (paperback 5.5x8.5in)
ISBN-13: 978-0-6488867-7-8 (hardback)
ISBN-13: 978-0-6488867-5-4 (e-book)

Available in paperback, hardback and e-book.

Book Cover Design by
Creya-tive Book Cover Design
www.creya-tive.com

*To my parents who have been there for me through thick and thin,
you have given me the strength and courage to follow my dreams.*

I love you Mum and Dad.

Ice Mountain Isle
Fort Mindir
Point Ice Twin Towers
Tyron
Kora
Lake Oric
Plymort
Point West
Igor Mountains

NORTH TOWER POINT
MYRDREYA
THE RIDGE PASS
MOUNT SEASIDE
MORVIK
ELVANOR FOREST
NIRDRA
DARK CASTLE
SOUTH TOWER POINT
ZALINDOR

One

TRIXIE

WITH ONE FOOT AFTER THE other, he zigzagged through the dense trees. His muscles contracted as he climbed over decayed fallen branches and leapt over intertwined roots. Weaving his way at full speed through the thick forest, I attempted to follow.

The trees swayed, and the ground blurred. *Was it fog obscuring my view?* I could no longer see him—the blur engulfed him.

I pressed my fingers into my eyes, rubbing in circles.

The fog cleared, but we were no longer standing in the forest.

His back muscles strained against the chains binding his hands above his head. His shirt, ripped and dirt-stained, lay discarded on the ground beside him. I stared in horror at the red streaks across his muscular back—blood.

Gasping, I bolted upright. A pool of sweat dripped off my face and down my back. My heart thumped behind my ribs, threatening to jump out of my body. I squinted, barely being able to see in the darkness. Gently pulling back the covers, I revealed Kieran's muscular back I was so familiar with—unharmed. The tightening around my heart slackened. He laid next to me, sound asleep. My eyes searched over his peaceful features—his eyelids twitching slightly, his breathing even.

With the back of my hand, I wiped the beaded sweat from my forehead and closed my eyes, releasing a slow breath. A dream. A nightmare. I forced myself to take slow deep breaths to slow my heart rate and calm myself. I checked over his back again; his skin was as smooth and tanned as it usually was—no cuts, no blood.

Sliding back under the covers, I allowed myself to drift back off to sleep.

"WHAT'S UP WITH you today?" Kieran questioned me after the fifth time I failed to block his spell.

Standing back up, avoiding his eyes, I said, "sorry, I didn't sleep very well last night."

As he stood there, oblivious to the pain and fear still coursing through my body from the nightmare, I couldn't help but shiver at the thought of it. The images replayed in my mind like a horror movie on repeat. I wasn't sure why I had such a dream, but I didn't want to burden him with it. He had enough to deal with — training me as well as a few new recruits.

"Maybe we should give training a rest for today?" He said, his arms hanging by his sides.

I shook my head, raising my hand for the sixth time, "no, I'm fine. I need the practise."

Concern laced his brows, but a moment later, another purple ball of energy flew at me. I side-stepped, but it seared my arm. *Ouch.* I hissed and clutched my arm with my left hand.

"Are you okay?" Kieran said, his eyebrows pulling in as he started toward me.

"It's fine," I held up my hand to stop him, "just a small burn." I shook my arm as if to shake the burn off my skin. "Again."

Raising his eyebrows, he stepped back into place.

"Seventh time lucky?" I chuckled.

The corner of his mouth quirked up. But it was as fake as my mother's love for me. I beckoned him with my outstretched hand. His ball of energy trekked across the room. I willed myself to focus on my magic—that burn hurt, and I didn't want another. Turquoise electricity erupted from my hand and encircled me, forming a perfect sphere. Blocking magic was an essential skill, but it wasn't as effective as a full shield by the gifted—like my father's.

His purple ball hit the surface and dissolved.

"Well done." Kieran grinned, but it didn't reach his ears.

"Again?" I relaxed, letting the sphere dissipate.

He shook his head. "I think we should take a break."

My chest tightened. Training kept me distracted from the nightmare and gave me an excuse not to discuss it. I reluctantly nodded, allowing him to haul me away from the training room. I knew he wanted to stop because I was distracted. But I wasn't ready to tell him. *Would I ever be? Would he take me seriously or think it's just a stupid dream?*

We strolled, hand in hand, through the breath-taking glass city. Myrdreya still had me awe-struck. Like I was walking amongst crystals—the way the sun hit the glass and it gleamed and sparkled. I never dreamed something could be so mesmerisingly beautiful.

"Trixie, pixie!"

A groan resinated up my throat. I would know that nickname was for me in any crowd. I turned to see my father beaming across the path at me. While it was so nice to have my father back again, I hated my childhood nickname.

"Hey, Dad." I said, my cheeks flushing.

He reached out and embraced me, like he hadn't seen me only yesterday. We got little time to spend together — I was in full training mode with Kieran.

"Hi, Kieran." My father said, keeping his eyes on me.

"Jay." Kieran said, giving him a curt nod.

"How's your training going?" My father asked me.

"Good, getting better every day, thanks to Kieran." I smiled, gripping Kieran's hand.

Kieran's mouth twitched slightly. He gave me a half smile. His hand felt clammy in mine. *Was my father making him nervous?* No. He doesn't get nervous. *Tense?* Yes. His shoulders were tense, the muscles defined and bulging under his skin. He clenched his jaw, creating tight lines on his face. *Why was he tense?*

"Well," my father shifted to his other foot, "I'll leave you to it. I'm sure you have a lot to do."

I glanced between my father and Kieran, narrowing my eyes. It wasn't just Kieran. My father's jawline was set like stone.

"Ok, see you later." I said, as he turned and strolled away.

My eyebrows creased as we continued along the path, our hands linked.

"What was that about?" I asked.

Kieran glanced at me, "what do you mean?"

"You were uncomfortable around him." My eyes rested on his.

His Adam's Apple bobbed as he glanced away momentarily before coming back to mine. "Jay killed my parents, remember?"

His breath was heavy. Voice thick. I stopped walking, pulling on his hand.

"I thought you forgave him?"

He swallowed. "I did."

"But…"

"I can't shake it out of my head." His eyes were sad.

I sighed, stepping closer. "How do I make this better?"

"You can't." He shook his head. "He was mind controlled. It wasn't really him. I have to come to terms with it. It's just going to take time."

I watched him for a moment. My chest rose and fell. He squeezed my hand.

"It'll be okay." He said, pulling me into his arms.

He was comforting *me*. My father murdered his parents, and *he* was comforting *me. How can he have such a kind soul?* I sighed.

"Come on," he pulled my hand to continue strolling.

We rounded a corner of a building and halted in front of Jake. My breath caught in my throat and I adverted my eyes, pretending something was interesting on the wall beside me. I could feel Jake's eyes burning into my pale skin, but I held my gaze on the patterned wall.

"Jake, you're back!" Kieran slapped him on his upper arm. "How was your trip?"

"Relaxing." Jake said. He turned away from me to Kieran.

I heard little of their conversation after that. I had been avoiding Jake like the plague for the past few months—it hadn't been difficult since he had barely been around. The day my mother attempted to take over Myrdreya, and I had released my father from her grasp, was also the day that the first person ever had witnessed me losing control—Jake.

I knew he hadn't betrayed my trust, otherwise Kieran would have told me by now. *Wouldn't he? Or does he already know and was waiting for me to tell him myself?* I swallowed down bile. *But how long could I keep avoiding Jake? How long could I keep my secret from Kieran?* My hands grew clammy, and I pulled my hand out of Kieran's and wiped them down my pants.

"Trix?"

The sound of my name tore me out of my thoughts and I peered over my shoulder at Kieran. I glanced around and saw Jake's burly back and overgrown dark hair as he strode away. I chewed my lip.

"Are you sure you're okay?" Kieran placed a hand on my arm.

I nodded, forcing a smile upon my face. "Yes, of course. Just tired."

He pursed his lips and thankfully dropped the

subject anyway. We began walking forward again as I glanced over my shoulder. Jake was looking directly at me; we locked eyes for a moment before I hastily turned away.

LEANING ON THE balcony railing, watching the sky turn from blue to amber and crimson, I allowed my mind to wander. Only a year and a half ago, my life had been very different. I had been a normal woman living her mundane life; working to live and living to work. The bills had to get paid somehow. Money—there didn't seem to be such a currency in Myrdreya. Labelled as missing—my face plastered all over the Blue Mountains, and my house emptied of my processions. The photo frame, with the last photo of Kiarra, was the only item I had recovered. My clothes, my laptop, gone. All my favourite books were gone—although I would one-day visit a bookstore and buy new ones.

My magic had grown since the day my best friend was murdered. I still thought about her every day; if the culprit was ever released from prison, I promised I would avenge her death.

Thump. Thump. Thump.

My heart skipped a beat as I was pulled out of my thoughts. I crossed Kieran's room. I had abandoned my room and now lived in his. He wasn't here though, not tonight at least. He had been called away on a secret mission that I wasn't allowed to know about. His respect for Demetri kept his missions a secret. Sometimes I felt isolated and left out, but Kieran reassured me that everything was fine.

A tall figure shadowed through the thick glass door. I gripped the handle and hoisted it open.

"Jake." My eyes widened in surprise, my stomach lurching.

"You can't avoid me forever." Jake said.

I sighed. "I know. I just don't know what to say."

"I do." He shouldered the door open wider and pushed past me into the room.

All right then. I bit the inside of my cheek and peered out into the corridor, but it was empty. I closed the door and turned to him.

"I've done some research on your power." His eyes were steady on mine. "It's elemental magic. It can be very dangerous if you don't learn how to control it."

I swallowed. "Dangerous, how?"

"You could kill someone, or yourself."

Air whooshed from my mouth as my chest tightened. I plopped myself down on the end of the bed. Killing someone was the last thing I wanted to do, especially Kieran.

"So, what do I do?"

"I know someone who can help you." He replied as he stepped forward, looking down at me. "She's not in the city. We would need to travel to her…"

I grazed my teeth along my lip. If I left the city, I would need to let Kieran know. My stomach squirmed. If I didn't tell him, he would find out anyway. *Maybe he already knew?* I clicked my tongue as my racing heart slowed.

"Is that where you have been?" I asked. "Traveling for information about me?"

He furrowed his brows. "When you put it like that, it sounds like I have been spying on you."

I adverted my eyes and shifted awkwardly on the mattress, playing with the blanket under my fingers. The soft mink a comfort on my skin.

"You should tell Kieran he would want to go with you to see this elemental."

"Elemental?" My eyes snapped back to his.

"Her name is Tori. She is a Soul Weaver Elemental, also known as a Soul Elemental."

I blinked. "What does that mean? I thought Soul Weavers were the only magical being?"

"Oh, we are." He raised his eyebrows. "Soul Weaver's with elemental powers are called Soul Weaver Elementals…like you."

I gaped up at him. "I'm an elemental?"

I thought I had learnt everything about my new life, but I'm more than just a Soul Weaver. I was a powerful one—well, of the sort.

"A rusty one." Jake teased, the corner of his mouth

lifting, and continued in a more serious tone. "Tori will help you learn to control and use your powers. First, tell Kieran. Then we will travel to see Tori."

So he hadn't told Kieran—I had time.

"I don't know…" I pulled on a loose thread.

"He needs to know, Trixie." Jake breathed. "I've known Kieran for a very long time. I know he will want to know and, trust me, he *will* support you."

Well, this was it. I had fought so hard to hide from the world, but now I had to tell Kieran if I wanted to learn to control my magic properly. Jake was right. Kieran needs to know. I didn't want to lose control around him and hurt him—or worse.

Two

TRIXIE

AFTER I RETURNED FROM A stroll around the city, I paced back and forth in the corridor outside Kieran's room—my room. My pulse thrashed in my ears. I sucked my tongue and shook my hands. I wiped my clammy hands down my pants. Curling my hand into a fist, I rubbed my knuckles against my mouth. My stomach churned, and I clutched at it with my other hand.

Shit. Shit. Shit. How was I going to tell him? If I didn't tell him, I was just as bad as him when he hadn't told me about my parents. What was worse, Jake knew. The hammering in my ears grew louder. If Kieran found out Jake had known before him...I wasn't sure what he would say.

Okay, Trixie, get a hold of yourself. Blowing out a series of quick breaths, I shook my hands out again. *You can do this.* I gripped the hem of my shirt, straightening the material, and stopped pacing. Releasing a slow breath, I stared at the cloudy glass door. *Okay, here goes nothing.*

I stepped forward and reached for the door handle. I almost gasped when it swung open before I could grasp it. Kieran stood in the doorway, the stray lock of hair dangled on his forehead—and he was shirtless. *Oh. My. God.* I blinked away the surprised expression on my face before he noticed. All the anxiety from a moment before evaporated.

"Hey, I was wondering when you would be back." Kieran's dazzling smile lit up his gorgeous face.

My cheeks flushed. "Was a nice walk around the city."

"That's good." He stepped forward, wrapping his arms around my waist, his hands resting on my lower back, and he brushed his lips against mine.

Stepping backward, he pulled me along with him into the room. Hooking the door with his foot, he pushed it closed behind us. In that moment, I had forgotten why I had been panicking outside the door for so long, and allowed him to distract my worrying thoughts as I curled into his arms like they were made for me.

MY EYES FLUTTERED open as I stirred. Sun shafts peered through the gap in the curtains. Pushing the blanket off my bodice, I glanced over at Kieran's smooth, muscular torso. My lips parted. *When was I ever going to get over how damned sexy he was?* Never, I hoped.

"Good morning, beautiful."

I snapped my eyes to his. *Fuck.* My heart jolted. *How long had he been watching me?*

"Morning." I mumbled, turning my body toward him, my cheeks glowing scarlet.

"I love when I catch you staring," he said, his head rested on his hands.

I ran a finger across his chest and down his stomach as I scooted closer to him. His hand found my hip and his lips softly touched my cheek. I licked my bottom lip and bit into the flesh as his eyes bore into mine—his tiny silver specks glinting in the sunlight. Teasing him, I circled my fingers around his lower abdomen, and then rolled away from him and climbed out of bed.

"Let's go practise the sphere shield. I want to get it under control."

He rolled his eyes and reluctantly nodded with a groan. "Alright."

Pulling my clothes on, the soft squeak of the mattress reached my ears. I peeked over my shoulder as he stood.

His muscles contracted as he stretched. I couldn't resist looking at his naked body.

He scooped up his own clothes and pulled them on. I watched as his muscles flexed. *How did I find myself in this entire new life with the most handsome man by my side?*

I shook my head and busied myself with my boots as he, too, started buckling his own on. He reached the door, grasping the handle, before I finished with the last buckle.

One foot after another, I moved over to him and out the door. Avoiding his gaze, I silently remembered what I was supposed to be telling him. I scraped a hand through my long platinum blonde hair, butterflies flying around my stomach. I bit my lip as he closed the door and we made our way through the castle and out into the harsh morning sunlight. It was still strange not feeling the warmth on my skin or a cool breeze while in Myrdreya.

The glass city never faltered; the beautiful carvings on the building walls, the unique never-growing trees, and the archway with the moving orbs to the training grounds—Myrdreya mesmerised my soul, inside and out, every time.

We entered the training grounds and found it vacant.

"No one's here." I stated.

He raised his eyebrows, "well, it is six in the morning."

"Oh, I didn't realise it was so early." I walked further

into the room to get myself positioned.

"Alright, since there is no one here, let's do something a little different." Kieran said as he strolled across the room toward me.

He stood beside me as I gazed at him, my eyebrows knitted together.

"I'm going to cast fireballs to fly around the room, and you are going to block them." He stated. "They will come at you from different angles, so this will teach you to block on the move and to be aware of your surroundings."

"How many are you going to create?" I asked nervously, my pulse picking up speed.

"Two to begin with, then will increase if I'm satisfied with your performance. You remember the word?"

"Revento."

"Good. Remember to practice in your mind, not out loud."

I nodded. "Ok, let's do this."

He smirked and cast two balls. They flew around the training grounds with no agenda. I watched as they passed us and looped around.

One energy ball turned and headed straight for me. I held out my hand, creating an energy ball of my own, which hit his and it disappeared. I searched around the room for the other and as it turned toward me. Throwing a ball at it, it exploded. I grinned.

"Good job." Kieran created four energy balls,

allowing them to fly rampart around the room.

I tried to track all of them, but I couldn't focus on all four. My pulse quickened.

"How I am supposed to keep track of them all?" My eyes flicked to each of the purple glowing balls.

"You won't. Just like when we are in combat, you can't focus on everything." He said. "Just focus on what is more threatening."

More threatening. Okay, easier said than done—they were all threatening. The closest ball circled around and headed directly toward us. I threw a turquoise ball at it—it exploded and disappeared. Turning toward the next closest ball, I also saw another closing in at the same time. My eyes flickered between the two—*focus on which was more threatening. Shit.* They were both coming at me.

I hastily cast one ball after another—sparks flew as they collided and burst apart.

"Good." I barely heard him murmur.

"Where is…?"

We both spun around and saw the last purple ball shooting toward us in full force. My stomach roiled and my lips trembled. I reached for Kieran's hand—our free hands shot up in sync, forming energy balls of our own.

Turquoise and violet enveloped one another, forming into one larger ball of energy. The two colours of electricity swirled around together, hitting the singular purple ball and bursting it into a million pieces.

Both of us froze in place for a long moment, the

silence deafening—besides the pounding of my heart in my ears.

"Did you see...?" I mumbled.

I wasn't looking at him, but I had seen his nod from the corner of my eye.

A whoosh of air escaped my lungs, and I turned to him. "Have you ever seen that before?"

"No," he stated, his eyes staring wide-eyed at the place the spheres had evaporated.

I studied his face, waiting for him to knock out of his trance. His eyes glazed over, his skin tort. I swallowed, taking a small step to close the gap between us, our hands still entwined.

"Demetri." He stated, and he pulled me along with him, striding out of the training grounds.

"What?" I blinked, my brows furrowing.

"If it's happened before, he will know."

He hauled me along through the city, not slowing down until we reached the spiralling ramp up to Demetri's room. We both stayed silent, walking hand in hand, side by side, around and around to the top platform.

We paused outside for a split second before Kieran knocked rapidly on the door. No answer. My pulse hastened and my palms began sweating. He raised his fist again and banged harder on the glass—I flinched. *Would break if he were to hit it with such a force?*

The door opened with a grumble.

"What in the name of — ?" Demetri began, but paused when he saw Kieran's wide-eyed features. "What's wrong?"

Demetri opened his door wider and Kieran pushed past him. I gave Demetri a sly smile before following Kieran into the room. He closed the door behind us, immediately turning toward us.

"Why are you storming into my room at this early hour? Are we under attack?" Demetri queried.

"No attack." Kieran shook his head.

"Then what's going on?"

Kieran hesitated. He glanced at me for a moment before settling his eyes back on Demetri's. I wiped my hands down my pants.

"We were in the training room, and our energy balls...well they kind of..." he was having difficulty saying it and I gave him what I hoped was an encouraging smile, "they joined."

Demetri's eyes widened.

"Joined?" he raised his eyebrows. "As in, the colours warped together into a larger sphere?"

We both nodded in unison.

"You've seen it before?" Kieran asked.

Demetri sighed. "Yes. My wife."

Kieran and I locked eyes for a moment. I moved to stand next to him, my fingers sliding into his.

"She and I could do the same thing. For some reason, our power was stronger together. We could join our energy together—red and yellow, which also made it glow orange. It was beautiful, like a ball of fire…like a tiny ball of sun…"

Demetri moved around the room and sat in his chair behind his desk. It was then I realised he was still in his nightwear.

"Kiri and I were unstoppable." His eyes were distant and empty.

I shifted uneasily beside Kieran. But he kept his eyes on Demetri.

"Together, we lead our army to fight. Everyone looked up to us." Demetri told his story in a daze; he gazed at the ceiling, remembering. "No one got in our way. Our combined orbs were fireballs of destruction. For the good, of course. No one dared to defy us; except for the Dark Soul Weavers."

His expression turned dark; it was almost like his emerald green eyes had gone grey with the anger that bore inside him.

"That was before she was taken from me," he spat, shifting his gaze.

We stood in silence for a long moment; I didn't take my eyes off Demetri's haunted ones. He stared blankly out the door, through the small gap between Kieran and I. The silence was becoming deafening as I grew anxious waiting for someone, anyone, to break it.

Demetri's body turned in his seat, and his intense eyes bore directly into mine.

"Your mother…"

My jaw tensed, teeth clenching together. I didn't want to hear anymore, but his piercing gaze had me locked on him.

"She took her from me. Kiri left me for the power your mother was going to give her."

I swallowed. "But she didn't give her power…"

"No…" he shook his head, "…she killed her. I didn't even get to say bye."

I tore my eyes away and stared at the ground. To have his wife torn away from him and not even able to say goodbye—I couldn't imagine the pain, the heartache for the rest of his life. No wonder he hadn't trusted me. *Did he still not trust me?*

"The fact that your orbs have joined together means your magic is much more powerful than we imagined." Demetri said, his voice light.

I raised my chin, looking back at him again. The anguish had vanished; his eyes were emerald again, allowing me to release a breath I hadn't realised I was holding.

Shifting my gaze to Kieran, he was already looking at me. With his expression full of love, he squeezed my hand. I squeezed back, and together, we stood staring at one another for a long moment.

WE STROLLED BACK to Kieran's room soon after, neither of us speaking. I assumed he was mulling over what we had just learnt, just as I was. We were so compatible that our magic even knew it; *unstoppable,* Demetri had said.

Kieran slid his hand into mine. The warmth was comforting. Magic kept throwing me surprises—Kieran, too, apparently. *Was elemental magic a mystery to him as well? Will he be afraid of me?* Surely not. He didn't appear to be afraid of anything.

I crossed his room to the balcony. Leaning on the glass railing, I looked over the city. His balcony was my favourite spot to ponder on my thoughts—except for the gardens, of course. I felt his warmth behind me before I saw him. I glanced over my shoulder, and Kieran slowly stepped up beside me. He placed a hand around my waist, the other on the railing.

"I didn't know such magic existed." Kieran mumbled, his fingers tapping on the railing.

"I never knew any of this existed." I swallowed the lump in my throat and stared at the horizon. The sun continued its ascent, casting a warm glow over the landscape. "I mean, how can such a magical world exist without everyone in the world knowing about it?"

His tapping stopped. "We've hidden it well. Hiding protects us. If we hadn't hidden, the hunters would have been able to recruit a lot more people and kill us off."

Kiarra's face swam in front of my thoughts. *Would she*

have joined them? If she had lived through that day, would she have feared me? It hadn't occurred to me before. My stomach knotted as the memories from that day flooded back to me. She hadn't stood a chance against that murderous man.

"Are you okay?" Kieran's voice broke my train of thought.

I wiped away the tears forming in my eyes and nodded. "Just thinking of Kiarra."

Kieran smiled weakly. "I'm sure you miss her."

"She loved reading fantasy novels. This world, this magic, it's just like a fantasy novel." I breathed. "She would have thought she was dreaming if she came here."

"Like you had." Kieran's smile broadened, and he nudged my cheek playfully with his nose.

I giggled. "Yeah, just like I had."

Three

TRIXIE

"I-I NEED TO TELL you something." I tucked my hair behind my ears.

His beautiful silver flecked brown eyes bore into mine expectantly. My chest rising and falling rapidly, I gazed into his eyes nervously. Air rushed into my lungs as I pulled at my fingers and chewed my lip.

"I can do s-something that I didn't know was m-magic." I stuttered.

He continued to watch me closely, his eyes raking over my face, "what is it?"

"I can manipulate my surroundings." My eyes flicked back and forth between his, watching for his a reaction. When he said nothing, only continued watching me, I went on. "I can warp the ground, the walls, anything solid around me. Jake called me a Soul Weaver Elemental."

Seeing the flash in his eyes when I said Jake's name, I bit my tongue. *Shit.* I shouldn't have mentioned Jake.

"Jake knows," he stated, his voice blunt.

I nodded. "Yes, but only because he saw it. I asked him not to tell you..."

His eyebrows pulled together. My stomach churned. I was digging a deep hole and I may as well jump into it. I swallowed hard. I wanted to go bury myself under the covers of the bed.

"How did...when did he see?" he asked.

I gazed over his features; he didn't seem angry, but unreadable. *Was he...jealous?*

"When I was the last in the dungeon, I-I lost control and he saw the entire room warped around me." I explained, hoping he would forgive me for not telling him sooner. "I wanted to tell you before Jake did, so I asked him not to tell you."

He nodded, but said nothing. His eyes glazed over as he stared at me. I bit my lip.

"You're not mad, are you?" I shifted awkwardly, rubbing my arms.

"No." He blinked and shook his head, letting out a

sigh. "But you could have told me earlier. I knew something was bothering you. I just couldn't work out what it was."

My thoughts jumped to my nightmare—he assumed my magic had bothered me, not by my nightmare. I chewed the inside of my cheek—I wasn't about to correct him. I was terrified by what the dream meant. *Was it real? Would it become real? Had I witnessed the future?* With the magical world that I was still discovering, anything was possible.

"Are you okay?" he asked.

Blinking, I stared at him for a moment before answering. "Yes, I'm just confused."

"We will work this out together." A smile tugged at his lips.

"Jake knows someone who can help me…" I trailed off when I noticed his smile fall from the mention of Jake's name.

"Tori." He breathed.

I furrowed my brows. "You know her?"

"She—" he hesitated, "she used to live in the city and left to live by herself."

Why he hesitated, I wasn't sure. *Was she someone important to him? Was she his ex-girlfriend?* I clenched my jaw and swallowed before stepping forward, placing my hand on his forearm.

"She can help me?" I searched his eyes.

"Yes," he sighed, "she can help you. The problem

is...we don't know where she is."

My heart sank, and I closed my eyes for a moment.

"No idea at all?"

He shook his head, sighing. "We need to speak to Jake."

There was an edge to his voice when he said his best friend's name. I ground my teeth; I hoped I had caused no tension between them. It wasn't my intention.

WE QUICKLY FOUND Jake in the training grounds—exactly where Kieran had said he would be, training. Only two pairs of Soul Weavers were here today. It was oddly vacant at this time of day.

We crossed the grounds, Jake's eyes locking on mine and I chewed the side of my tongue as we approached him—an expression of understanding crossing his face. He turned to Kieran, forehead slicked with sweat. He wiped the back of his hand across it.

"We need to talk," Kieran said, then lowered his voice, stepping closer, "about Tori."

Jake's eyes flickered to mine, then back to Kieran, and he nodded.

Jake turned back to his opponent. "Good job this morning, Quinn. We will have to call it there for now. I have an urgent matter to attend to."

"Okay." Quinn said, his shoulders slumping.

"Maybe this afternoon we can have another round."

Jake said, patting him on the back.

Quinn's face lit up, and he grinned. "Okay! See you then!"

Jake turned back to us. "Let's go somewhere private."

Ten minutes later, we were sitting in Kieran's room on the plush lounge. Kieran gripped my hand and was making circle motions with his finger on the back of my hand. Jake sat across from us in the armchair.

Jake heaved a sigh. "So, you told him."

I nodded. Kieran shifted beside me, his circles pausing, and I squeezed his hand. It felt impossibly hot in the room as the tension in Kieran's body grew.

"We need to find Tori." I said.

"You and me both." Jake mumbled. My eyebrows drooped and opened my mouth to speak, but Kieran cut in.

"We've already been looking for her." Kieran said. At first I thought he spoke to Jake, but then he twisted toward me. "It's like she's disappeared from Zalindor."

I searched his eyes, my stomach dropping, and said, "she disappeared? Wait...what's Zalindor?"

"Oh," he said, his eyes flicking to Jake for a moment. "I never actually told you the name of this land, did I?"

My eyes widened. "Zalindor is the name of the...realm we're in?"

A bellowing laugh escaped Jake's lips. I tore my eyes from Kieran and glared at Jake. *What was so funny?*

"You think we're in some kind of other dimensional

realm?" Jake laughed again.

My cheeks heated. "Well, where else would we be?"

Jake stifled his laugh with difficulty. "In the middle of the ocean, maybe?"

I stared at him blankly.

"Zalindor is a large island in the middle of the Pacific Ocean." Kieran explained, drawing my attention back to him. "Myrdreya is the glass city of Zalindor, and there are many forests and other towns across the island as well."

"But it's not even on the map." I furrowed my brows, thinking back to the Atlas maps I had seen in the past.

"No, it's not." Kieran said. "Because you've been looking at the mundane maps, not the Soul Weaver maps."

Kieran stood up and crossed the room to a drawer. Sliding it open, he rummaged through the draw for a few seconds before pulling out two folded pieces of paper and returned to the lounge. He unfolded one of papers and placed it on the small table in front of us. The map was hand drawn with ink with such delicacy. It was beautiful. Kieran pointed in the middle of the ocean that was labelled the Pacific Ocean. And there, at the tip of his finger, was an island drawn with the word next to it: Zalindor.

"Wow." I let out a breath of air. "But, how has...non-magical people not found it?"

"Everything you see on this island was magically

built from the floor of the ocean thousands of years ago." Kieran explained.

"No way…" I whispered.

"Yes way." Jake said, humour gone, leaning back in the armchair. "Soul Weavers used to live among mundanes, but we were feared and hunted. It got too dangerous, so our ancestors sought to find a new home."

"So, they built one. Far out in the ocean that mundanes wouldn't find." I said. "But don't ships pass through and see it?"

Kieran shook his head. "There are wards all around the island, which deter the ships away so that no one would accidentally stumble across it. The only way in or out of Zalindor is to portal to Myrdreya. This way, we can monitor who is coming and going."

"That's amazing." I shuffled my feet, my mind going back to the day I had arrived in Myrdreya. "But, wait…Levi was ported to Zalindor, and you didn't know it. And all those other Soul Hunters…"

"That," Jake sighed, "is a mystery."

Kieran swallowed and cleared his throat. "It's ancient magic. Magic that was thought to have died with our ancestors…"

"Thought to have died?" I asked, my brows furrowed.

He glanced at Jake and back at me. "Until Tori…and you."

"I-I have this ancient magic?" my mouth hung open.

Kieran nodded, watching my reaction closely. I gazed absentmindedly around the room, sucking on my lower lip.

"It was thought that Tori might be a descendant." Kieran said, bringing my attention back to him.

"So everyone knows about her power?"

Jake shifted, and I glanced over at him.

"Not everyone." Jake said. "But a lot of people here in Myrdreya do, yes."

"You don't think…" I took a breath and started again. "She didn't let them in, did she?"

"No." Jake's stern voice blasted in my ears—louder than he had intended, from the moment of shock crossing his face.

Kieran and I stared at him for a moment.

"No, we don't believe she did it." Kieran confirmed. "She has a very pure heart. She would never betray us like that."

I nodded and stared down at the map. All this time, this island had been right there. And, I…I had ancient magic. Surely they were mistaken. My eyes flickered to the second paper.

"What's on that one?" I asked, indicating the folded paper in Kieran's lap.

Kieran picked it up and flattened it out on the table on top of the other map.

"Zalindor." He said.

A gust of air left my lungs, and I stared at the

drawing of the island. There was a smaller island in the north-west, covered in white, named Ice Mountain Isle. A lake in the south-west that was half the size of Ice Mountain Isle, named Lake Oric. Igor Mountains resided to the east of the lake along with a dark castle on the other side of the mountains. A long mountain range ran through the middle of Zalindor, with only one obvious passageway through it. Then, there were several forests and small towns around the island. I spotted the forest we once traveled to in my early days of arriving in Myrdreya, Elvanor Forest.

I marvelled at how big the island looked on the map and I had only seen a small part of it. My eyes gazed over the clouds in the top right corner of the map and I pointed at them.

"Myrdreya." Kieran answered my unasked question.

"They didn't want to draw it?" I asked.

"Apparently drawing a floating glass city was too hard." Jake cackled, and I cracked a smile. "However, they had reason to not draw it. If a mundane was to find these maps, the city wouldn't be exposed."

I nodded. "Right."

"So, we have been looking for Tori all over Zalindor." Kieran said. "No trace of her so far."

"The last place I have been looking is in the Ice Mountains." Jake said.

My eyes gazed over the smaller island in the top left corner of the map.

"That's where you were while you were away," I stated, "looking for her."

Jake nodded, lowering his gaze to the ground—I could see his heart was aching.

"Ok, so, where haven't you looked we should go?" I asked.

Jake's eyes flicked to Kieran briefly. "The tallest mountain on Ice Mountain Isle."

Kieran looked up at Jake. "You think she could be there? Right up in the freezing snow?"

"She loved the snow." Jake whispered, and Kieran shared a wistful smile with him.

"I guess we're going snow hiking!" I said, raising my eyebrows.

⊱≼≼≼◉≽≽≽⊰

MY SHOES MADE no sound on the stone floor. The damp coldness of the corridor crawled over my skin. A shiver ran down my spine as I walked along in the darkness, only vaguely aware I wasn't alone.

A scream sounded ahead, echoing off the walls. I bolted forward, my shoes still silent on the ground. Turning a corner to the left, I stopped in front of a metal door with a tiny window.

Swallowing down my bile, I creeped forward and placed two hands on the door. I leaned forward, lifting the shutter on the window and peered in. A small empty stone room on the other side. I tried the handle, and it clicked open. I released a rush of air and pushed the door wide, revealing the stone room wasn't empty anymore. My breath hitched in my throat.

Kieran was sprawled on the cold floor, his hands and feet tied. Dirt and blood marked his face and bare skin. His eyes were closed.

"Kieran?"

My voice echoed around the room, but he didn't move. I bit my lip and stepped forward, reaching my hand out to him. Another scream sounded, and I spun around.

I gasped, bolting upright in bed. I looked over at the man beside me. Kieran was sound asleep. Sighing, I closed my eyes, dropping my head backwards. *Breathe, it's just a dream,* I told myself. Opening my eyes, I adverted my eyes from the ceiling and I froze. I stared wide-eyed around the room. The glass walls had warped, bulging out in triangular shapes toward the bed.

I snapped my eyes shut again. *Breathe in…and breathe out. Again. Breathe in…and breathe out.*

My pulse slowed as I took slow deep breaths, telling myself over and over to relax and breathe. After a few minutes, I peaked through one eye and sighed. I opened both eyes and looked around the room—back to how it should be.

Sweat matted my hair and soaked my clothes. I climbed out of bed, heading for the wardrobe, and pulled on a clean singlet. I crept back to the bed, flipping my pillow over and laid back down.

Finding Tori was a priority now. I couldn't allow the warping while I slept. Had I not awoken when I had, who knows if those spikes had gone right through Kieran?

Tori—I had to find her.

Four

KIERAN

DEMETRI HAD GIVEN TRIXIE HER first mission, and she seemed on edge. At sunrise a knock on the door woke us and a messenger had informed me of our mission and handed me the details in a letter. Trixie peered over my shoulder to see her name sprawled at the top with mine.

Kieran and Trixie,
Report to the portal room at 5:30am and meet
with Jake and Clara.

Go to Swansea, Tasmania, Australia and find a sixteen-year-old girl named Sienna. Her powers are growing and she's scaring the mundanes. Bring her back to Myrdreya.

Demetri

The letter had a full address sprawled at the bottom.

Half an hour later, we were meeting Clara and Jake in the portal room.

"Morning!" Clara said as we entered.

"Morning." I said.

All four of us wore our black battle gear. Clara, Jake and I all equipped daggers on our belts and inside our jackets. Trixie had one simple dagger on her belt that I had presented her with this morning. It was very short, with a tapered blade coming to a sharp point. The hilt as long as the blade itself.

I gave her a quick lesson on how to hold and use it if the need arose. Minutes later, it was sheathed, and we were hurrying through the city.

"Let's get moving then." Jake said, nodding to Mae.

Mae stepped forward and opened a portal to the small town in Australia.

THE DARK OMINOUS clouds hid the stars and moon. Our shadows cast long behind us as we strolled toward the streetlight on the corner of the suburban road.

I reached out and gripped Trixie's hand, giving it a squeeze. She gave me a soft smile, but I could see the nerves written all over her face. Her eyes bulged and the fingers on her free hand were twiddling with each other.

"So, how did Demetri know about this girl?" Trixie asked.

"We've got connections in the human world." Jake said.

"What sort of connections?"

"Some Soul Weavers prefer to live with non-magic folk." I answered. "So, they keep us up to date on any mis happenings."

Trixie nodded. "So, what do we do?"

"We find her." Jake said as we passed under the street lamp and turned down the street.

"And we find out what she knows about her magic." I explained further.

Trixie's jaw tightened. "And take her back to Myrdreya to train her? Like you did with me."

"Precisely." Clara said.

We walked up the dark street; street lights only every fifty metres. The lack of dogs barking or occasional owl hooting in the distance set my teeth on edge. But, we were in an outback small town, so it must be the norm here. *Right?*

We turned a corner and continued up the next street.

"Thirty-four," Jake muttered as we passed a house on

the left, the numbers painted on the wooden fence.

"Here." Clara said.

We turned to see *thirty-three* in silver metal digits on the brick letterbox. Beyond the grass hedge, the double-storey house was built out of dark grey bricks with the odd light grey here and there. Old-fashioned shutters covered the windows and the front wooden door had a white paint with a dark grey frame.

"We'll go through the back. You take the front." Jake whispered.

I nodded once and moved toward the front door with Trixie by my side. Jake and Clara disappeared around the side of the house.

"No car out the front." I whispered. "Her parents mustn't be here."

"So, we're just going to take her away from her parents?" Trixie whispered back.

I took a deep breath and studied her face for a moment. "It's not like that. She's a danger to them."

Trixie arched an eyebrow, and I turned back toward the door. Reaching out, I sent sparks from my hand into the door lock. It clicked, and I pushed it open soundlessly. We stepped over the threshold, into an entryway that lead toward the dining room and kitchen. A doorway on the right lead to the lounge, which was empty. Another doorway to the left lead into another hallway and stairs.

I pointed up to show to Trixie we were going upstairs.

At this time in the morning, the girl would surely be sleeping. The hairs on the back of my neck stood on end, my senses subdued—I couldn't feel any presence nearby, except Trixie, who followed me closely.

We took one stair at a time and stopped briefly at the top stair. I could see only three doors leading from a short hallway. One door stood ajar and was obviously the bathroom. The other two doors were closed.

I crept toward the door on the left first. Slowly turning the doorknob, I pushed the door wide open to reveal a room with an empty bed and dresser in it. The bed had been neatly made, and someone had kept the room tidy. No one had been sleeping in it tonight. I scanned the room and checked for hiding places. Empty. The room was oddly lacking belongings or traces of anyone being here recently.

My brows furrowed, lips tight, as I exited the room and creeped around the corner of the doorway, keeping to the shadows. The door opposite us stood ajar, and I peered through the darkness of the hallway.

Trixie walked slowly behind me, her eyes squinting. We crept closer to the door until we were outside of it. Slipping a dagger from my belt, I gripped the door handle, pushing it open, and stepped in.

My shoulders stiffened as I jerked my head back. "Levi?"

Trixie peered around the door frame, leaning on my shoulder, frowning. We both stared at Levi standing in the opposite corner of the room.

"What are you doing here?" Trixie said beside me.

Levi's eyes flicked between Trixie and I. "I was about to ask you the same thing."

A crash from downstairs echoed through the house. Something shattered.

Gripping Trixie's wrist, we both abandoned Levi in the room and made our way back toward the stairs.

"Come, now, Sienna." A deep voice drifted up the staircase. "We will teach you how to use your powers."

"I know how to use them. Haven't you seen what I have done?" A girl's voice said.

"Yes, you have made quite the show." Said a third huskier voice.

"Well, I don't need your help then, do I?" Sienna sneered.

"You can become more powerful if you join us." The deep voice said. "We will show you magic beyond your knowledge. She will give you the guidance you need."

Trixie and I glanced at each other. There was only one 'she' they could be talking about.

"Dark Soul Weavers?" Trixie whispered.

I nodded and whispered back, "we need to stop them before they take her."

Trixie visibly swallowed and nodded. We crept down the stairs, eyeing the floor below. I listened to where the voices were coming from—it was difficult when my senses weren't working properly.

"Who is *she*?" Sienna asked.

I pointed toward the left, motioning to Trixie that the voices were toward the lounge room.

"You will meet her when you come with us." The deep voice said.

Looking up the corridor, I saw Jake and Clara pressed up against the walls outside the doorway to the lounge room. Pressing a finger to my lips, I motioned to Trixie to keep quiet as we moved along the hall.

Crunch.

Clara and Jake whipped their heads toward us. *Fuck.* I paused and adverted my eyes down. Lifting my boot carefully, I stared at the broken glass scattered across the floor.

"What was that?"

"I definitely heard something."

"Go check it out."

I stared wide-eyed ahead at Jake and Clara. We agreed silently that it was now or never. Jake and Clara stepped into the lounge room and I rushed forward, ignoring the cracking of glass under my boots. Trixie hurried close by me and we entered the room behind them.

"What—." A black-haired man didn't get to finish his sentence as Jake and Clara hit him in the chest with fireballs and he collapsed.

A second man stood on the opposite side of the room in front of a girl whose raven black hair draped loose over her shoulders—the candle light subdued her sapphire highlights. A rough beard adorned his dark face, emerald green magic sparked at his fingertips.

"Who are you?" His husky voice demanded.

"You're outnumbered. You don't get to ask the questions." Clara said.

Jake and Clara stood a metre or so in front of me. Trixie stood just behind me, peering over my shoulder, her light breath in my ear.

"Trix, watch him." I pointed to the knocked out man on the ground. "If he wakes…you know what to do."

Trixie visibly swallowed, eyeing the unconscious man, then nodded. I stepped forward to join Jake and Clara.

"Sienna, are you alright?" I asked.

"Of course." Sienna's ice-blue eyes scanned me up and down, then looked over at my comrades.

"This man is lying to you," Jake said. "You don't want to go with him."

The bearded man laughed. "She would be worse off going with you."

"Who are you people?" Sienna said, her focus alternating between the bearded man, the conscious man, and us.

"Ignore these imbeciles…come with—." The bearded man said before being cut off.

"Shut up." Clara blurted.

Jake watched Sienna. "Please, Sienna. Come with us.

We'll protect you and teach you the proper ways of magic."

"Oh, please." The bearded man spat. "You will teach her to create a shield, but not to fight for herself."

"Don't listen to him." I said. "We will teach you to defend yourself and how to attack safely."

"I don't need your help," Sienna said, her hands in fists as she stepped away from the corner. "I can defend myself fine, and I know how to use my magic."

"Using it to knock that lady over and catch her on fire?" Jake said. "Yes, we can see you can use it."

"But you don't have control of it." Clara said. "We'll help you control it."

"They'll help you suppress it." The bearded man grumbled.

Sienna whipped her head around and eyed all of us. Fury, fear and confusion lit up her eyes. I wasn't sure which was more fearsome. Ruby red sparks licked her fingertips. Some gold sparks joined the red and circled around her palms.

My mouth gaped open slightly. It can't be. Jake glimpsed over at me and back to the young girl. Sienna was oblivious to the power she wielded—the magic of the ancients that was thought to be long gone.

While Sienna was distracted looking at the bearded man, I stepped backwards and paused before she would notice the movement.

The bearded man continued to bicker with Jake and

Clara, drawing Sienna's attention to them. I stepped back slowly and carefully, and took Trixie's hand. She tore her eyes away from the unconscious man and searched my face.

"Trust me." I whispered in her ear. "Together, shield spell."

I didn't know if it would work. But I knew if we didn't try, Sienna was going to kill us all.

Five

K IERAN GRIPPED MY HAND AND pulled me close to him—the pleasant scent of cedarwood and lavender whisking up my nostrils.

"Be ready." He whispered, his lips barely moving.

I studied his face from the corner of my eye—his jaw tense, eyes locked on Sienna. My heart pounded in my ears as I waited for Kieran's signal.

"STOP IT!" Sienna screamed.

Everyone ceased their bickering and turned to her.

Our eyes widened as we all stared. I hadn't noticed the fire growing up in her arms and blazing in her irises until now. The magic that grew within and outside her body was both mesmerising and terrifying. Tremors ran through my muscles. My pulse thrashed in my ears as I struggled to listen to their conversation.

"What the…" the bearded man stepped backwards.

"Sienna." Kieran lifted his free hand toward her. "You are losing control. You need to calm down before you kill us all."

Clara whipped her head to Kieran, her eyes searching his face quickly before pivoting back to Sienna. She grabbed Jake's wrist and tugged backwards. Together, they stepped slowly backwards towards where Kieran and I stood.

Her hair caught alight, but the strands didn't burn. They whipped around like fire. Her skin blackened on her arms; her hands were already charcoal.

"Sienna, please." Kieran begged. "We can help you control that. You just need to relax and calm down."

"No one can help me." Sienna said, her nostrils flaring. "I killed my parents. Can control of my magic bring them back?"

My lips parted. She was grieving from the loss of her parents. A loss at her own hands. My heart ached for her. I chewed my lip.

"I'm sorry about your parents," Kieran said.

"What am I?" Sienna said through gritted teeth.

"You're a Soul Weaver, with ancient powers way beyond your knowledge."

She narrowed her eyes. "Ancient powers? My parents had *no* magic."

"It must have laid very dormant in your bloodline for thousands of years. And it's finally awoken in you."

"Oh, how lovely. I have ancient powers from descendants I never knew, and there's no one even alive that can teach me." Sienna spat.

"I didn't know anything about my magic." I said.

All eyes turned to me. Kieran squeezed my hand—he silently pleaded with me.

I swallowed and continued. "I have special magic that needs to be controlled, and I still need to learn how to control it. Like you. They are helping me. They can help you, too."

Sienna eyed me over. I shifted uncomfortably next to Kieran. The flames engulfed her arms and started down her chest.

"How can I trust you?" Sienna asked. "I don't know you. I don't know *any* of you."

Her chest heaved. Her wild eyes glared at us. My throat tightened, and I attempted to swallow the lump resonating there.

"You're young." I said. "Don't throw away your life."

"Don't act like you know me!" Sienna blurted out, and she opened her arms wide as the flames engulfed her body.

"NOW TRIX!" Kieran thundered.

In unison, Kieran and I put our free hands up, forming fireballs at our fingertips. Jake and Clara stepped slightly behind us, ready to attack, but froze.

Our fireballs entwined together and then a swirl of turquoise and purple spread out into a shield surrounding us. The four of us stood in the dome and stared at the fiery figure in front of us. The bearded man stood frozen by the wall, staring in horror.

Sienna's electric swirls of fire sparked off her body. She screamed as the ruby red and gold engulfing her — her screams were horrifying.

Kieran and I stood our ground with our hands outstretched, putting all of our strength into the shield.

The fire set the room ablaze, enveloping the shield. Between the licks of flame, we watched as a massive hole blasted out of the side of the house. The walls were blackened with soot and Sienna was gone.

I gasped — the shield collapsed. A heavyweight bore on my body. My bones liquified, legs turning to jelly, and I wobbled. Kieran slipped his hand around my waist, allowing me to lean on him. The bearded man stood burnt to a crisp against the wall. Turning around awkwardly, I stared at the other man — he, too, blackened beyond recognition.

"She…" I breathed, "she exploded."

"You tried." Kieran said, his hand squeezing my side gently.

"We tried." I corrected.

Kieran merely nodded.

Jake and Clara gazed around the room. There was no trace of her being here except for the burnt room, the hole in the wall, and the two dead men.

"We need to go," Clara said.

Kieran tore his eyes away from me. "Yes, let's get out here before someone comes to investigate."

⁂

WE STEPPED OUT of the portal, back into Myrdreya. I breathed in the fresh air, relieved to be rid of the smell of burnt corpses.

"So," Clara said, "did you want to tell us what happened back there?"

Kieran's arm was still wrapped around my waist to keep me steady. He led me outside. Clara and Jake followed, and we stood in a small huddle outside the portal room in the sun.

"Well, Sienna was a lot stronger than any of us imagined." Kieran said.

Clara shook her head and rolled her eyes. "You know that's not what I'm talking about."

"Your magic joined." Jake stated, his voice blunt.

Kieran and I glanced at one another.

"Yes." Kieran said. "It's happened before, by accident. I don't really know what it's called. Demetri didn't say."

Clara's eyebrow shot up into her forehead. "Demetri knows about it?"

Kieran nodded. "He could do the same with his wife."

"So, what does it mean?" Jake asked.

"Demetri said our powers are stronger together." Kieran shrugged.

"That explains how you managed to shield us all. Only someone with a shielding gift should have been able to do that." Clara said.

Kieran nodded. "Incredibly rare."

"So, how did you know Sienna was going to explode?" Jake asked, his eyes flickering from Kieran to me.

"I've read what has happened in the past when ancient magic wielders lose control." Kieran said, glancing at me momentarily. "I could see her losing it."

I shifted beside him and said, "how did you know our shields would combine?"

"I didn't." Kieran mumbled.

I stared at Kieran's face. His eyebrows were furrowed. Clara and Jake warily glanced at one another.

"You didn't?" Clara said.

Kieran shook his head. "She could have killed us all. We had to take a chance that it would work."

"Well," Clara sighed, her lips curling at the corners. "Thank you for saving our lives. Both of you."

Kieran bowed his head slightly, and I gave Clara a

small smile. My smile faltered quickly when I remembered who else had been in the girl's house.

"Levi was there." I muttered, more to myself than anyone.

Kieran's hand moved from my waist and rested on my lower back.

"Levi?" Clara's eyebrows raised.

"I couldn't sense him." Jake said.

Kieran frowned. "I couldn't sense anyone in that house."

"Why was Levi there?" I said, my voice sounding distant.

All eyes were on me. Jake, Clara, and Kieran stayed silent.

"I don't understand." I continued, frowning at the ground. "He left Myrdreya to find a normal human life…and then he shows up at Sienna's house."

"I doubt I need to say this…" Jake cleared his throat, "but he lied to you."

I snapped my eyes to Jake's face and bore into his. There was only pity in them.

"I'm sorry, Trix." Kieran said.

I tore my eyes away from Jake's and looked at Kieran. He appeared to want to say more, but thought better of it and closed his mouth.

"You agree?" I asked Kieran. "You think he was there with those men?"

Kieran sighed. "I don't really know what to think."

Silence fell between us. We stood looking at each other for a long moment. A few Soul Weavers passed by us, paying us no mind.

"I better report to Demetri." Jake said, breaking the awkwardness. "Let him know we failed."

Kieran nodded. "I better get Trixie back to the room to rest. That was a lot of magic for her."

I adverted my eyes to the glass ground. Jake was right. We had failed. I had failed. My first mission and I had failed.

Six

I SHIFTED ON THE GARDEN bench, crossing my ankles. "Dad, I need to ask you something."

"Sure, Trixie Pixie."

"Dad…" I groaned, "I'm not a child anymore."

My father chuckled. "Of course, sorry. Old habits."

We sat in silence for a long moment. Light faded in the distance as the sun cast a red and orange hue on the clouds.

"So, what did you want to ask?" my father turned to me, stretching his legs out in front of him.

I sucked in a lungful of air and let it out in a whoosh.

"What happened the day you and mum…" I couldn't finish my question.

"Left?" he finished.

I nodded. *Abandoned me was more the wording that crossed my mind.*

"I hate thinking about that day…" he scratched his neck and sighed. "Your mother said we needed to go to Myrdreya and save it."

"Save it?"

"Yes, it was in danger of being investigated by humans and being destroyed." He laughed awkwardly. "She lied, obviously. She wanted to take over it, have all Soul Weavers follow her."

"So, humans don't know about Myrdreya?" I asked, watching the last glow on the horizon.

He shook his head. "No. Well, only Soul Hunters do. But they don't have access to get here."

"Levi got here, and so did many other Soul Hunters."

"Yeah…your mother ported them here." He frowned. "I think they are still here…somewhere."

Still here somewhere. Yes, they had to be. I hadn't believed my mother had given up. She was in hiding—planning something. We just didn't know what or where. Why Demetri had allowed to escape was still a mystery.

I frowned. "Wait. How did she port them here when Myrdreya is the only place you can port into?"

He scratched his beard. "I don't know."

My shoulder slackened, and jaw clenched. *If he hadn't known, how would we?*

"The day we left, the day I left you…" his voice cracked, "was the worst day of my life."

I gazed at the sky, keeping my eyes on the twinkling that started appearing.

"I didn't know what she had planned for months. I followed her blindly. I…I loved her."

I glanced at him and saw a tear drop from his eye and roll down his cheek. My lips parted, and I placed my hand over his on the bench. He breathed in and wiped the tear away, giving me a weak smile.

"What did you do when you found out?" I asked, my eyes returning to the night sky.

"I left."

"What?" my eyebrows shot up my forehead and I stared at him.

He nodded slowly. "I didn't get far. She found me."

"And then she controlled you?"

"Yes." He said, frowning. "Then she controlled me with that awful spell. I was trapped in my own mind for years, forced to do her bidding…murder his parents."

"Why?" I asked. "Why did she want them dead?"

He shook his head. "I don't know."

"She never told you?"

"She might have…but, I…" he stared ahead and fell silent.

The sound of boots drew our attention to the ramp

into the garden. Kieran strolled toward us.

"I thought I might find you here," Kieran said, his eyes locked on mine, his expression unreadable.

My father smiled up at Kieran, "I'll…ah…let you two…"

He kissed me on the forehead and stood. He nodded once to Kieran and left the garden. Kieran raised his eyebrows at me and seated himself.

"Is everything alright?" Kieran asked as he searched my face.

"Mmhm." I tore my eyes away and gazed back at the stars, now twinkling brightly in the darkness. "I thought we would see the Milky Way here, but I'm yet to see it."

Kieran chuckled. "Nice change of subject."

I bit my lip, hoping he would let my change of conversation slide.

"We do see it here, but most of the time it's hard because of the light reflections from the glass." He explained.

I nodded. "Makes sense."

We sat in silence for a few minutes. Kieran scooted closer to me and wrapped his arm around my waist. His touch was always comforting. I leaned into him.

"So, what were you and your dad talking about? It looked quite serious." He said.

Damn. I thought I had successfully swayed him from talking about my father. I swallowed down the growing unease in my stomach.

"Not much." I said casually. "I asked him about the day they left me."

I filled him in on the discussion, but I left out the part about his parents. I hadn't got an answer from my father, anyway.

"I still don't understand why they didn't take you with them." Kieran said, and he reached up to tuck my hair behind my ear.

Shaking my head, I said, "I don't know...maybe because I didn't have magic then."

"Possibly. Although you always had magic, it just hadn't awoken yet."

"They probably believed I didn't have magic at all."

"Still, that's no excuse to leave your daughter behind." There was a rough edge to his voice, like he was angry on behalf of me.

I cleared my throat. "Nothing we can do about it."

"No, I suppose not." His fingers drew circles on my thigh, sending tingles down my leg.

"I suppose we should..." I glanced sideways, the corner of my mouth perking up. "Are you tired?"

His hand slid to my inner thigh, teasing. "Not at all."

Sucking on my lip, I slid my hand over his thigh and onto his bulge, already semi-hard.

"I guess we should go back to the room, then." I whispered.

"We should." His lips grazed my neck and my breathing grew heavy.

I stood and gripped his hand, hauling him from the garden.

⁂

"DEMETRI WASN'T HAPPY about Sienna." Jake told Kieran and I the next day.

"Well, it wasn't like we didn't try," Kieran said.

Jake nodded.

Kieran looked at Jake sharply. "Did you tell him about her ancient magic?"

"Yes, of course."

"Such a waste." Kieran muttered. "She could have been so powerful to overthrow Julianne."

"Or too powerful for us to even train." Jake said, flopping down on the lounge in Kieran's room. "She was wild. I don't think anyone could have trained her and controlled the power she processed."

I sighed. "She was too young."

Kieran nodded. "Yes, she was too young. But Jake is right. She probably would have crashed Myrdreya out of the sky."

"True." Jake said. "Probably a good thing she blew herself up."

I shook my head and walked out onto the balcony. I didn't want to think about her blowing herself up. Too young to throw her life away like that—whether or not she did it on purpose. I couldn't help but wonder if she would still be alive if we hadn't arrived there. My stomach flipped and chest tightened with my heart racing in my ears.

"Are you okay?" Kieran said as he stepped up beside me.

"Just can't stop thinking about her." I said. "If we hadn't gone there, then maybe she would be—."

"No." Kieran interrupted me. "She may still be alive if we hadn't turned up, but she would be with Julianne and trained to kill instead of to save."

Taking a deep breath, I looked out over the city. Even the beauty of the city couldn't take away the pain of the girl's death.

"For all we know, she might have sacrificed herself to save everyone from her." Kieran said. "Either way, she was dangerous to keep alive with that much power."

"But, you could have trained her," I said, "right?"

He nodded. "Yes, but it would have been risky. She accidentally killed her parents. Imagine what she could have done here."

I sighed and nodded, turning to him. "I guess she is at peace now. The memory of murdering her own parents would have haunted her."

"Exactly." He took my hand in his. "There wasn't anything more we could have done. So, don't blame yourself, okay?"

I nodded. Jake was still lounging inside, not looking at us. I glanced over at Jake as he shifted his weight to cross his ankles.

"I need to see Tori." I stated.

"Yes, we need to," Kieran said, "as soon as we can."

"It can't wait much longer." I said, bringing my eyes back to his.

Kieran's eyes searched my face, and he asked, "what is it?"

"I-I keep having nightmares and wake up, finding the room warped. I could hurt you while we sleep."

Kieran's brows furrowed. "Why didn't you tell me?"

"I didn't want to worry you." I said, my mouth grew dry.

"Let's go tomorrow." Jake's voice drifted out to us.

I shouldn't have been surprised that Jake could hear us. While he was allowing us time together on the balcony, he was in earshot.

"Tomorrow?" I repeated.

"Yes, I'll get permission from Demetri for us to leave tomorrow." Kieran agreed.

I nodded. Somehow, it was relaxing to know we would be on our way the next morning to get the help I needed. I would finally learn to control this elemental power — if we could find her.

Seven

"I'M SORRY, KIERAN. I can't grant you permission to go, I need you here," Demetri said, sitting behind his desk.

"Why?" I demanded, my shoulders tight, hands clenched in fists. "There's plenty of other capable Weavers!"

"Not ones I trust as much as you." He said. "Jake will keep her safe on his own."

I heaved a sigh and paced the room.

"They could be weeks—months!" I dragged a hand

through my freshly washed hair with a huff.

"I'm sorry," Demetri said, "but that's my final answer."

I shook my head and stormed out of the room, making my way back down the spiralling ramp. *How could he refuse me?* For everything I had done for him, I had thought he would allow me this. *How was I going to deal with being away from her for so long?* I wouldn't know how the training was going or if she was hurt, or if they had found Tori at all. Gritting my teeth and flexing my hands, I headed back to my room.

After entering, I slammed the glass door, a resounding boom echoing through the room. I glimpsed back at the door; luckily the glass was made of reinforced thick glass or it would have shattered.

Trixie stood by the wardrobe halfway through putting her belt on. She stared at me, eyes brows raised.

"He refused." I said, answering her unspoken question.

"What?" Trixie eyed me blankly, her jaw slackening.

"You and Jake have permission to go. I have to stay."

"But—."

"I know." I closed the space between us in a few quick strides, taking the belt from her hands and finished buckling it around her waist. My eyes found hers and I whispered, "you still have to go."

Trixie bit her bottom lip. *God, I love when she does that.* I grazed my fingers softly along her jawline to her chin.

My thumb traced over her lip, my eyes following the motion. She jerked away from my hand as a knock sounded on the door and we both stared at the shadow through it.

"Come in." I called out.

The glass door swung open and Jake walked in, dressed in black fighting gear. He stopped a few paces in—his eyes flickered from me to Trixie. His shoulders dropped, his jaw clenching.

"What's wrong?" Jake asked.

"I don't have permission to go." I said.

"How can he refuse her getting the training she needs?" Jake blurted.

I shook my head. "You and Trixie have permission to go alone. I have to stay."

Jake took a deep breath and let it loose with a big whoosh. He pinched his nose and groaned.

"It will be okay." Trixie said, sliding her fingers into mine. "I will have Jake and Tori once we find her."

Jake let his hand fall from his face and nodded. "I'll keep her safe."

"I know you will." I said with a small smile.

"We better get moving," Jake stepped backward toward the doorframe. "I've already let Mae know."

Grinding my teeth and nodding, I turned to Trixie and whispered, "stay safe."

"I will." Trixie said, squeezing my hand.

"Stay close to Jake."

Trixie nodded. I handed her the thick winter black jacket hanging on the wardrobe door and she slipped into it, zipping it closed. I gripped the jacket, pulling her against my body. There was a soft click behind me, and I knew Jake must have left to give us some privacy.

She held me in her arms as tightly as I held her. Neither of us wanted to break the embrace. We both knew it was going to be a long time before we saw each other again. A long time apart that neither of us wanted. My eyebrows creased as I scanned her face before tucking my head down beside hers.

"I wish I was coming with you." I whispered in her ear.

"Me too." She whispered back, sighing.

"I don't want to be away from you. I don't know how long it's going to take."

She pulled back, keeping her hands tightly around my neck, her fingers playing with my hair.

"I love you, Trix." I said. "I'll be here waiting for your return."

A soft smile spread across her mouth and she cupped my cheek with her hand, her beautiful blue eyes boring into mine.

"I love you, too."

I pressed my lips to hers. She parted for me so I could slip my tongue in. The sound of her moan sent adrenaline down my body, and I bucked my hips into hers. My hands found the zipper on her jacket and I shoved her jacket off within seconds. Gripping her waist tightly with one arm, I lifted her against me — she wrapped her legs around me.

"I. Need. To. Go." she said between the passionate kisses I pressed on her lips as I moved over to the bed and sat her down on the edge.

"Are you sure you have to?" I said as crouched down on my knees, sliding my hand down her stomach and in between her legs.

"Jake is waiting." She breathed.

Rubbing my hand against her, I said, "he can keep waiting."

Another moan escaped her, and she rocked her hips back and forth. She gripped my shoulders, digging in her nails. I pushed off the ground and leant over her, kissing along her jaw and down her neck. Her hands moved down my arms to my hips. One hand stayed on my hip, the other slid down to my bursting bulge, already hard and waiting for her. She pulled at the sides of my pants and tugged them down. Her hand gripped me, stroking up and down.

She gasped. "I want all of you."

"Now I can't let you go." I whispered, hastily unbuckling her belt.

Sliding my hand behind her back and lifting her bottom off the bed, I pulled the belt off and unbuttoned her pants. She wriggled to assist to take them off. I threw her pants and underpants on the floor and finished removing mine.

The moment my pants were off, she grabbed my waist, and I lowered my body between her thighs. Her hand wrapped around my hard cock and she stroked it with the perfect amount of pressure and speed.

I lent on an elbow, kissing her neck and sliding my hand down between her legs again—so moist. She moaned in my ear and I nibbled at her jaw. My mouth found hers and I sucked on her bottom lip.

She rocked her hips into my hand and I slipped two fingers inside, rubbing her clit with my thumb. Sliding my fingers out, I smoothed the moisture over her clit and settled my fingers on either side of it, rubbing gently. Her breathing grew heavy, her hips rocking harder against my fingers.

Her grip around me hastened, and I moaned against her mouth. I wanted to be inside her. I wanted to feel her around my cock.

She let go of me, her hands gripping my hips, nails digging in. I lowered myself, moving my hand from her wet pussy and teasing her with my tip, sliding along her. Her nails dug harder, and she moaned against my lips, rocking her hips. She pushed herself against me, the tip sliding in.

We both held each other tighter, my mouth smashing into hers in lust. I pushed in further and she bucked up against me. We moved together, faster and faster, sweat slicking our skin.

She moaned, not attempting to keep the sound down. "You feel so good."

"Tell me more." I breathed as I thrusted in and out of her.

"I want—all of you," she panted, "deeper."

"You have me." I thrusted in as deep as I could go and she let out a loud sensual scream.

She shuddered against my pulsing cock and together we came.

Eight

STEPPING OUT OF MAE'S PORTAL, I immediately threw my arms up to hug myself. Even the thick woollen undercoat of my jacket wasn't keeping the chilly air from freezing my skin. I sensed Jake's presence as he stood next to me, the only warmth nearby.

Looking out over the view before us, I was mesmerised. A mountain terrain lined the horizon before us, covered in a white forest, and a beautiful ice lake met the bottom of the mountain range. A blanket of snow stuck to everything. I looked down at my shoes to see them covered in freshly powdered snow.

I blinked. "So, this is…"

"Ice Mountain Isle." Jake said. There was an edge to his voice.

The icy island in the top right corner of the map swam into my mind. I glanced out of the corner of my eye, the tension in Jake's jaw prominent as he gazed over the landscape. The water was almost entirely frozen over, except for the middle—I assumed the deepest part of the lake. Snow had fallen recently, leaving no clear path around the lake.

"This way." Jake said, starting his trek through the soft snow.

I fell into step with him. "She lives here?"

"Somewhere. I have been searching for her for the last few…years."

"So, you said you don't know where she is," I hesitated, "but you think she could be here?"

"To an extent," he said as we struggled through the fresh snow. "I've explored these mountains, except that one."

I followed his pointed finger to the tallest of the mountains across the lake. I swallowed. The peak had my neck craning to look up at it. I had never been to the snow, and now I was about to climb a monstrous mountain covered in it. *Excellent.*

"So, why didn't we portal to it?"

"Because she would sense it." Jake said. "Less chance of her knowing we are near if we walk."

I grumbled to myself as we trudged north-west through the fresh snow around the lake's edge. The mountain drew closer, and I grew more anxious. As time ticked on, I was thankful for the sun overhead, warming my body so I didn't get frost-bite. I shuddered at the thought—toes turning black and falling off—no, thanks.

After what felt like hours, we started the ascent of the mountain, leaving the frozen lake behind us to the south-east. Tilting my head up, I gazed over the cloud covered sky in search of the enormous ball of fire. The sun was nowhere to be seen. I shivered, rubbing my gloved hands together. *So much for the warmth.*

The frosted pine trees had icicles on their branches, with fresh snow on the leaves. The higher up the mountain we climbed, the larger the icicles were. We rounded a rock face and the sound of trickling water reached our ears.

"Waterfall?" I questioned through my chattering teeth.

"If that's what you call it, sure." Jake jutted his chin up toward the flowing water.

I followed his gaze and saw the so-called waterfall, quickly understanding. The waterfall was mostly frozen over. Minuscule streams flowed down and along a creek bed. It was only a shortfall, but it was the true beauty of snow, ice, and water together.

I stared at the magnificent sight. Kiarra would have absolutely loved this; she adored waterfalls. I always thought that she would one day get married in front of one. But that day never came. My chest tightened—my heart aching to see her again.

"Come on." Jake said lightly, jolting me out of my thoughts.

I took one last look at the falls and followed behind Jake as he began a steep climb up a rocky surface. Thankfully, it wasn't vertical. After almost slipping several times and Jake catching me around the waist, we clambered over the top of the sloped, rocky ground, and it levelled out. *When would we be there?*

After endless hours of trudging through the thick snow and up the steep rock faces, my muscles ached, screaming at me to stop. *I cannot stop,* I told my body. *Just a bit longer.* This was for me, for Kieran. The dense air, thick with moisture, reached my lungs and I coughed. The snow stuck to our boots as we trudged through the trees. Falling forward, onto my hands, I looked down to see I was knee deep in the soft snow. Cursing, I wriggled my feet in an attempt to free myself.

"Are you okay?" Jake grabbed me by the arm and heaved upward; I staggered out of my white sinkhole, collapsing in his arms.

"Thanks, I'm fine." I mumbled, stepping out of his arms and brushing the snow off my legs. "Are we close?"

Jake looked ahead into the trees, his eyes scouting the

area. "I think so."

"You've got no idea, do you?"

Jake sighed and shook his head, "not exactly. She's around here somewhere though. We just need to look for signs."

"Signs? There's signs to her house?"

He shook his head again, a slight husky laugh in his voice, "no not that sort of sign, and she doesn't live in a house."

My frosted eyebrows pulled together as shivers ran through my body. "Then how are we going to find her?"

"She lives in this forest with a glamour, I'm sure of it." He said as we stalked onwards. "She used to always talk about the snow."

"What's a glamour?"

"She's warped her surroundings to keep hidden from the world." He glanced over his shoulder at me. "She's created a glamour. If we didn't know what to look for, we could have passed by her already without even knowing it."

"But I don't know what I'm—."

I froze and stared at a nearby trunk of a large pine tree. The frosty snow sitting on the bark shimmered in waves—I had to blink several times and refocus to make sure I was seeing it correctly.

"What do you see?" Jake asked from beside me; he glimpsed in the direction I was staring, his brows furrowed.

"That tree," I pointed to the tree trunk, "it's moving."

Jake looked over the trunk carefully, his eyes narrowing.

He shook his head. "I don't see anything."

I slowly stepped forward, out stretching my hand to touch the shimmering bark. Even through the gloves, I could feel the off warmth touching my freezing fingertips as I ran my hand over it. The bark moved in waves as I pushed my palm against it—my hand disappearing into the tree trunk.

I jumped backward, ramming straight into Jake's chest. His arms held my shoulders to steady me as we both stared at the place I had touched.

"What... is that?" I asked through breaths of cold air.

"Tori," his voice was barely a whisper.

He released me, stepping around me, as he cautiously moved toward the tree. He reached his hand out to touch it. The shimmery ripple widened; like a ripple across a lake, it grew outward as the tree warped. Jake froze, staring ahead. Branches twisted away in waves, the trunk split open like a curtain, revealing a beautiful cavern filled with sparkling coloured lights. The cavern wasn't empty, though.

A beautiful young woman, no older than thirty, stood before us. Her skin looked so pale against the dark candlelit cavern, and her amber eyes glowed. A pale green silky dress hugged her curves; it had several thin straps crossing over one another, across her collarbones and over her shoulders. Her long, almost-white hair flowed freely down her back. My mouth gaped, and I blinked rapidly as I stared mesmerised at her beauty. I realised she wasn't wearing the appropriate attire for the snow—at all. She wasn't even wearing shoes.

Tori, I assumed she was, barely noticed me; her eyes were locked on Jake. He couldn't take his eyes off her, either. *Was I missing something here?* I stood awkwardly beside him, desperately wanting someone to move or say something. I waited another a moment before the silence deafened me.

"I'm Trixie."

Tori tore her eyes away from Jake and settled her piercing glare on me. I instantly regretted speaking, wanting to recoil back like a snake.

She flicked her eyes back to Jake, her voice as menacing as her eyes. "What are you doing here?"

I recoiled. Her voice was just as menacing as her eyes.

"I'm sorry, if there was anyone else…" He trailed off, clearly not wanting to finish.

She narrowed her eyes at him slightly before turning back to me. She looked me up and down; I felt too casually dressed to be meeting with this elemental. I shifted to the other foot, stretching my back as I moved. For a moment I thought she was going to shoo us away, but she jutted her chin upward.

Jake glanced at me quickly before stepping through the tree trunk doorway into the cavern. I followed, turning to watch as she held up her hand and the doorway rippled back shut again—closing us in. The inside of the invisible doorway was solid bark; you wouldn't know it opened if you hadn't already seen it.

"How did you find me?" Tori asked, still in the blunt tone.

"A lot of traveling," Jake said. "Snow was always your favourite."

Tori jolted slightly. It was clear that she wasn't impressed he was here. Whatever had happened between them, it had left a scar on them both.

"I would ask again why you are here…" she glanced at me, "but I think I already know."

Jake nodded and swallowed.. "Please, she needs training to learn to control her powers."

Tori's eyes darted toward him. She was so beautiful, yet fierce. She turned her back on us and walked down a skinny hallway I hadn't noticed before. As she walked, she pointed with her finger and lights appeared on the ceiling, lighting her way; they looked like little stars in the night sky. Her magic was stunning. *Was creating light her gift?*

Jake gestured for me to follow. We followed her in single-file through the hidden cavern; the opening behind us warped and closed, closing us deeper in the secret place. I couldn't believe this cavern was inside of the tree—and she had created it.

The hallway opened out into what appeared to be a

very empty living room; sticks warped into the shape of a lounge chair on one side and a table with a single chair on the other side. She clearly never had visitors, and by the looks of the empty surroundings, she owned little either.

Tori stopped in the hallway on the opposite side of the room.

"Wait here," she said, before disappearing down the hallway.

Jake glanced around the room, his face blank with emotion. My eyes were drawn to the ceiling—it was twinkling with tiny stars, one glowing like a moon. There was just the right amount of light in the room to see clearly. A gentle light—calming.

"There's a room down the hall on your right." Tori's voice made us both jump out of our thoughts. "One room to share. I can only do so much magic at once."

Jake and I shared an awkward quick glance before moving toward Tori. She stepped aside, allowing us to pass.

"Thank you," I said, offering a small smile.

"I will organise dinner," she stated as she moved toward another room off to the left that I hadn't noticed before.

⚜

"SO, DO YOU want to tell me why she appears to not want you here?" I asked after a very awkward silent dinner, raising my eyebrows.

I plopped myself down on the make-shift bed. It wasn't the soft mattress back in Myrdreya, but it was better than sleeping in the snow.

Jake sighed as he sat on his own bed, across the cavern room from me. "We have history."

"What sort of history?"

He avoided my gaze, clearly not wanting to answer my question.

"The kind that aches your heart to talk about," he said, shifting his body to lie down.

He crossed his ankles and slid his hands under his head, staring up at the ceiling. I understood. My heart ached with his as I remembered Levi. *Had he found his happiness?* I wouldn't know. I smiled slightly to myself, hoping that he had. My smile faded. He had been at Sienna's house. *Why had he been there?* I looked back over at Jake to find him staring at me.

"She and I had a connection," he said, pain in his chocolate eyes, "until she lost control of her elemental power and..."

I tilted my head slightly, showing him I was listening. Instead of finishing his sentence, he stood and pulled his jacket off. I blinked, confusion lacing my expression. He pulled up his shirt, revealing his stomach. My lips parted. I had to use all my self-control to not jump up and start shooting furious questions at him.

"What happened to you?" I breathed, eyes wide.

"She accidentally warped a gate into my stomach. I almost died," he said, covering his deep scars. "She never forgave herself. She left, told me to never look for her, and she locked herself away from the world so she couldn't hurt anyone again."

I swallowed. "I don't know what to say…"

"You don't have to say anything. It was an accident. But it damaged her more than it damaged me."

"But she almost killed you." My eyebrows raised.

He nodded. "Yes, but some days I wished I had died instead of living without her."

Tears welled in my eyes. "I'm so sorry."

"Me, too."

He laid back down on his bed, staring back at the ceiling. I allowed myself to lie down too, lying on my side. Jake rolled over, facing the wall. He had clearly finished talking.

Our room didn't have a door; I was partially glad. It made me feel more comfortable sleeping in the same room as Jake. I dropped my eyes and looked out of the room into the hallway. Tori was leaning against the wall, peering around the corner at me. Our eyes locked—she must have heard our conversation. Her blank expression was unreadable. A moment later, she pushed herself off the wall and walked away.

Nine

TRIXIE

"SO, LET ME GUESS, YOUR magic comes alive when you're upset?" Tori asked across the breakfast table the next morning.

The night had been rough. Sleep hadn't come easily for me, nor had it been comfortable lying on a bed made of sticks.

We awoke in the morning to see Tori had redesigned her table and added two chairs to occupy the three of us. A small, but kind gesture.

Arching my back to stretch it out, I said, "yes, or

when I'm anxious."

Tori nodded, her expression blank, but I could see she understood. Jake sat beside me; the air between them was full of tension. I picked at the bacon and eggs on my plate, attempting to ignore their awkwardness.

"Ok. I will help you." Tori said after what felt like half an hour of silence.

I lifted my eyes to look at her, relief spreading over my body.

"I can't make any promises that you will succeed, but we can only try." She looked down at her empty plate.

"Thank you." I sighed.

She bowed her head before standing to collect our plates and clear the table. Glancing at Jake, I could see his eyes trailing Tori as she walked back to the kitchen.

"How long do you think it would take?" I asked, tearing my eyes from Jake's.

The clang of plates being set down in the sink reached our ears. Tori rinsed the plates and cutlery, not answering me. *Had she heard my question, or was she ignoring it?*

When the water turned off and Tori wiped her hands on a towel, I opened my mouth to question again.

"How—?"

"I heard you the first time." Tori's voice wasn't unkind, but it still set me on edge.

Was it a mistake coming here? We clearly weren't welcome. Tori could kick us out at any moment and we would be back to square one.

"To answer your question," Tori said, walking to a hook with a thick woollen coat on it. "How long will it rain for?"

"Pardon?" I stared at her, blinking.

Tori sighed. "It might rain for a day or it might rain for weeks."

Why on earth were we talking about rain? I shook my head, my brows pulling together. Eyeing Jake, I hoped he understood my confusion. He looked amused.

"It's like the saying, *how long is a piece of string?*" Jake's mouth quirked up in the corner.

My heart sank. "So, we could be here for weeks?"

"Or months." Tori said, shrugging into her coat.

If my heart could actually sink out of my body, it would have done just that. *Months away from Kieran?* I had hoped it would be days, maybe a week.

"Let's see what we're working with." Tori stated.

At my blank expression, she continued.

"Get your jacket. We're going outside."

I stood from the table and fetched my jacket from the room. When I returned, Tori stood awkwardly by the hallway as Jake walked towards her.

"Tori…" Jake began.

"Okay, Trixie. Let's go." Tori ignored Jake and headed down the hallway.

Jake stared after her, and I bit my lip, walking over to him. I gave him a weak smile, and he held his arm out, indicating for me to go ahead. I stepped forward, following behind Tori, faintly aware that Jake was close behind me.

⚜

"ALL RIGHT," Tori said after we had been walking in silence through the snow for about fifteen minutes, "this should be far enough away."

"Far enough from what?" I asked.

"My house." Tori said. "The last thing I want is for you to tear down my home."

I shifted on my feet, hugging myself. I definitely didn't want to destroy the only thing she had left. The cold bit at my skin through the jacket, even with the slight warmth of the sun peeping through the clouds.

"So, tell me more about it." She asked.

I swallowed. "Well, I used to only warp the walls around me when I was upset. But lately it's been happening when I'm asleep."

"Asleep?" Tori raised her eyebrows.

I nodded. Jake moved to a nearby boulder, settling himself down. *Was he anxious that I would accidentally warp our room through his body while we slept at night?* I shuddered at the thought.

"Did you wake up thinking about something in particular? Were you dreaming? A nightmare?" Tori questioned.

"Yes, dreaming." I frowned.

"Are the dreams always the same?"

"Not exactly the same…"

"But…" Tori pressed, twirling her hands in a motion for me to continue.

I sighed. "They are always about Kieran getting hurt."

She nodded. "So, you obviously care about Kieran and are scared of him getting hurt. And end up dreaming about it, upsetting you in your sleep, and so the emotions then take over and warp your surroundings."

"Um, yeah, I guess so." I said, looking deeply into her eyes.

I thought I saw a flash of recognition, but it was gone as quickly as it came. *Had I imagined it?*

"Okay, I want you to use the memory of those dreams as fuel. Think about how you felt in the dream and when you woke up." She said.

My lips parted as the previous dream came to the forefront of my mind. The cold stone corridor and the small dark room Kieran had been in. I swallowed the lump in my throat.

"Close your eyes and keep thinking about the fear you felt," Tori said.

My eyes closed. My hands loosened around me, and I allowed them to drop to the sides of my body. The memory of Kieran on the cold, hard stone ground swam in front of my eyelids. My heart raced and sweat pooled on my hairline, even though it wasn't remotely hot on the cold mountain.

"Open your eyes," Tori whispered.

I blinked my eyes open and stared around me. Trees bent over toward us, branches stuck out at odd angles. I gasped and spun as I looked at Jake. He still sat on the boulder, but his shoulders were stiff and eyes wide. Branches curled around him. None of them touched him. They were circled around him as if they had avoided him.

Tori followed my gaze, and her lips parted. We watched as the branches retreated and the trees stood tall once again.

"Interesting." Tori said, still looking at Jake.

Jake's eyes were locked on Tori.

"Why did the branches circle him like that?" I asked, taking my eyes off Jake.

"You were protecting him." Tori said, a sadness in her eyes.

"How?"

"You subconsciously wanted to protect him from getting hurt."

I opened my mouth, but no words came. I had only been thinking about Kieran. *How had I been thinking about protecting Jake, too?*

"Your magic somehow knew you needed to protect him."

I frowned. "But what about you?"

"What about me?" Tori asked, her brows etched together.

"You wouldn't have wanted to hurt to Jake, but your magic did."

Tori paled. *Shit. Why did I say that?* Tori turned away from me and trudged off into the trees. My body turned rigid and my mouth fell open.

"I'm sorry, I—."

"Don't." It was Jake's voice that reached my ears.

I clamped a hand over my forehead. Tori walked a few more metres before she stopped beside a tree and sank against it. Her back turned from us. *How could I be so insensitive?* The words escaped my mouth before I even thought about what I was saying.

❧❀☙

THE HIKE BACK to Tori's home was awkward and silent. When we returned, Tori stalked off to her room, leaving Jake and I staring after her.

I ruined it. There could have been a chance for them, and I had to open my idiotic mouth. *What if she won't teach me now? What if she sends us away tomorrow?* My chance to learn control was gone. I would go back to Myrdreya, back to Kieran, with no way to stop it from happening.

My heart thundered in my ears. My body shook. I chewed my lip and tears welled in my eyes. My eyes closed as panic rose within me.

"Trixie?" Jake's voice was far away.

How would I ever learn to control it? I could go to sleep

tonight and impale Jake. I could dream about Kieran again and actually hurt him next time.

"Trixie." The sound of my name whispered from Jake's lips beside me.

I kept my eyes shut tight. My hands trembled at the sides of my body.

"Trixie, listen to me."

A cry escaped my lips. I reached my hands down, feeling the rough flooring around my boots. *Wait...when had I crouched down?* A wetness ran down my cheeks.

A hand touched my shoulder. A welcome warmth. But I refused to open my eyes.

"Trixie, you're okay." Jake said, his hand making a circular motion over my shoulder.

"No, I can't do this." I cried.

"You can! It will take time." He said.

I wanted to believe him, but my heart ached. *What if I tried and failed? What if I hurt him or Tori while training?*

"Trixie, you need to look at me."

"I can't."

"Yes, you can," he said, the circles continued on my shoulder. "I believe in you. You have to believe in yourself, too."

A strange laugh escaped me. "Believe in myself?"

"Yes." Jake breathed. "Now, open your eyes. We can work through this together."

I shook my head. My heart pounded in my ribs, threatening to break free. Broken. I had to be broken.

There was something wrong with me, something wrong with my magic.

"Come on, Trixie, together." Jake said.

His hand found mine and gripped it tight. I almost flinched away, terrified to hurt him.

"In the count of 3, open your eyes and look at me," he said, squeezing my hand.

"1…"

My body trembled all over. I wanted to find a dark hole and stay there forever.

"2…"

His voice was calming, but there was a hint of alarm in it. I breathed heavily through my nostrils, my chest heaving.

"3. Look at me, Trixie."

I sucked in a sharp breath and snapped my eyes open. My eyes widened in horror. Branches had grown out of the walls all around us. Sharp thorns lined the wood and threatened to tear us apart. The room was barely recognisable. It was a tangle of thorns like an overgrown rose bush — yet there were no roses.

My eyes locked on Jake's. He was huddled close to me, thorns inches from us. I mimicked the fear in his eyes, although he was focused on me.

"Trixie, calm yourself down," he whispered. "You can't do this alone. You always have someone around you that can help you through this."

I kept my watery eyes on his as I strained to listen

while the branches still grew and twisted around us.

"Kieran will be by your side. He will do everything he can to help you learn. You can do this. You will learn to control it."

Jake's face was so close to mine, we breathed on each other.

The branches stopped moving, a thorn pressed into my cheek. Jake didn't take his eyes from mine and I held his gaze. He nodded ever so slightly. My breathing softened and my heartbeat slowed.

The thorn in my cheek was becoming painful until it wasn't. It left my skin as the branches retreated into the walls. The room warping back to normal again. Jake released a sigh of relief and I collapsed into his arms and sobbed.

"You're okay." Jake said. "We're okay."

"Tori?" I pulled myself out of his arms and eyed the hallway.

Tori stood at the far end of the hallway, watching us—physically unhurt. Her expression was—again—unreadable.

Ten

KIERAN

A FEW DAYS HAD GONE by since she had departed. My eyes drifted to the empty sheets beside me—it was strange waking up each morning without her.

I climbed out of bed and pulled my pants on. Looking over my shoulder at her side of the bed, loneliness creeped up inside. My heart ached to know if she was okay. Allowing her to go with Jake alone was much harder than I had expected. Not that I didn't trust her, but it was the longest time we had spent apart, and if she was in trouble, I wasn't there to save her.

An envelope caught my eye on the beside table. My brows furrowed as I reached for it and opened it.

Kieran,

Meet me in my tower when you wake. It's urgent.

Demetri

It wasn't often that I received a letter to summon me; it was usually one of the other Soul Weavers or a guard that gave me the message.

Pulling a shirt over my head and boots on my feet, I exited the bedroom and headed off down the hallway. Quinn bounced around a corner in front.

"Hey, Kieran."

"Hi, Quinn." I said, as I continued walking, keeping a brisk pace.

He followed me through the front doors of the mansion. "Any training today?"

"Maybe later on this afternoon."

"Great! Can't wait!"

Quinn bounded off down a pathway to our left as I continued toward Demetri's tower. I shook my head, smiling; he was always so cheerful.

Shadows cast over the city. I glanced up at the darkened sky; light rain showered down, dissipating on the shield.

When I reached the tower in the middle of the city, I hurried up the spiralling ramp and knocked on Demetri's door.

"Come in," Demetri's muffled voice reached my ears.

I pulled the door open and stepped inside.

"We received this note this morning." Demetri handed me a crumpled piece of paper with a brief note scrawled across it.

Scanning the first three words, I blinked and re-read it. My heart dropped as I continued reading.

We have Trixie.

Kieran must come alone to the cliffs south-east of Morvik at 2pm today or she dies.

"Why didn't you wake me?" I blurted out as I read the last word.

"You can't go until 2pm. It's hours away." Demetri said, waving his hand in the air.

"Who took her? Who left this note?"

"A messenger boy. Quinn was scouting with Tayla when he appeared and gave him this note."

I raised my brows. "He just appeared?"

"Apparently so." Demetri sighed.

My eyes narrowed. "I saw Quinn on the way here. He didn't say anything."

"I told him not to. Look, I don't think you should go. It could be a trap."

"I'm not risking her death on it *maybe* being a trap." I spat and started pacing the room. "It has to be Julianne."

"I don't know," he sighed again, folding his hands in his lap.

"I won't abandon her if she's in trouble."

Demetri nodded, scratching his chin. "If you decide to go, be careful. You don't know what she's capable of."

I stopped pacing, and my eyes narrowed at him. "And you do?"

"I've known her a lot longer than you."

My lips pressed together, and my chest tightened. "I won't abandon her." I repeated and left the room.

THE DAY DRAGGED by as I watched the rainfall grow heavy, then ease. Clouds dispersed, and the sun traveled from one side of the city to the other. 2pm couldn't come faster.

At 1:30pm, I headed to my room and dressed in my black protective fighting gear. I clipped the knife sheaths to my belt and slipped my daggers into them. I pulled on my jacket and tucked another two daggers on the inside.

At 1:45pm I headed for the portal room. Not surprisingly, Demetri was already waiting at the entryway for me.

"So, you are going?" Demetri asked as I approached.

"Did you think any less?" I said.

He sighed and followed me into the portal room. "No. I knew you would."

I stepped forward.

"Cliff south-west of Morvik please, Mae." I said to the portal keeper.

Mae raised her hand, and moments later, a portal swirled in front of me. A lush green forest on a small cliff next to the crushing waves of the ocean.

"Be careful, Kieran." Demetri said.

"I will."

"I don't want to send a search party after you."

I raised my eyebrows, gazing over my shoulder at him. "So, you'll send a search party after me, but not her?"

"We've known you for a much longer time, Kieran."

"Yes, well, she's far more valuable." I half mumbled as I stepped toward the portal.

"More valuable together, I would say."

Pausing, I glancing back at him. Our magic joining, I had almost forgotten. I nodded to him once and walked into the portal.

⬥

IT WAS WINDY on the cliff I stood on. The ocean waves bashed against the cliff face below, spraying salt into the air.

"Hi there." A bored voice came from my left.

Tearing my eyes from the view, I whipped my head toward the man leaning against a tree. He had brown hair tied back in a ponytail and eyes the colour of oak. He had a dagger in one hand and he appeared to be cleaning under his nails with the tip of the blade.

"You must be Kieran," he said, his eyes drifting up

and down my body.

"Yes." I said, slowly moving my hand to my belt. "Where is Trixie?"

He sighed. "Ah, Trixie."

I eyed the trees beyond him. With all the training I had had over the years, I should have been able to track anyone nearby with ease. But there was nothing, not even animals.

"Well, you see…"

Something was wrong. *Why couldn't I sense anything?*

"She's not here." I blurted out.

The man pushed off the tree. "You can't sense her."

"You're blocking me?" I narrowed my eyes, my pulse quickening.

He shrugged. "Well, can't have you running straight for her, can we?"

"What do you want? An exchange for something for her?"

The man laughed as he stepped closer. "No, no. There's no need for an exchange."

"Let me see her!" I demanded, my hands in fists at my sides.

"In due time, my friend."

"I'm *not* your friend." I said through gritted teeth.

He shrugged again. "Nevertheless…"

A movement to my left caught my eye, and I reached for my dagger and turned. Something metal clobbered me in the face, and a head-splitting headache tore through my temple.

"Shit." I hissed and swung my dagger around, catching the man that smacked me on the forearm.

Staggering, I bolted for the cover of the trees. Rodents scattered, a snake slithered, and birds took flight as I approached — all living things I hadn't sensed. *I had to get away from these men.* I climbed over fallen branches and zigzagged through the trees. Not sparing a glance backward, I focused on moving forward, away from my pursuers.

SMACK.

"FUCK!" I grabbed my nose, leaning over.

What the hell? I reached my other hand out in front of me. My fingers flattened against the air. They've trapped me.

"Was a nice try." A snicker came from beside me.

I straightened, turning my head toward the man leaning against the nearest tree. *How did he always surprise me?*

He raised his eyebrows. "Invisible wall. Figured you would run, I was right."

"What do you want with me?" I wiped the blood from my nose, thankful it wasn't broken.

He smirked, a satisfied, menacing smirk. "You're going to have one hell of a headache."

"Already do." I muttered.

"More so then."

Something slammed into the back of my head. *Not*

again. I fell sideways. The metal smacked me again and everything turned dark.

⊱⊰

AN EARTHY, MUSKY smell tickled my nostrils. A faint hint of rotten flesh made me wrinkle my nose. Cautiously, I opened my eye lids a crack, but could see nothing. Darkness. Very aware that I was sprawled on a hard surface, but I had no idea where.

I listened, but could only hear a distant dripping of a liquid on metal. *Blood?* My heart pounded against my ribs, threatening to jump out of my skeleton. I had to keep calm.

A door slammed, making my eyes snap open. Searching the space in front of me, I couldn't see anything but black. *Had they blinded me?*

"Ah...you're awake, good." A heavy voice sounded.

I squinted through the darkness, trying to find the speaker. Footsteps came closer, then stopped. *Another person?*

"Leave us." An unfamiliar voice said, this one more raspy.

"Yes, sir." The heavy voice said and then there were light footsteps that grew further and further away.

Something clicked. The door latch. The room seemed to be slowly lightening as my vision returned. From the sounds of the voices, the footsteps and the door, I must be on the floor. I allowed my finger tips to search the ground where they were tied up. It was hard, uneven—stone.

"Kieran."

I tensed. *Who are these people?*

"Where is she?" I croaked.

"Who, Trixie? Not here. She was never with us…you fell into a trap. It was just too easy to capture you."

My blood turned cold and my heart sank. Demetri had been right. It had been a trap and I let myself fall right into it. I should have known better.

"You know she ran away with Jake…together. They planned it all along." The raspy male voice said casually.

"Nice try." I choked out, trying to sit up, but my ankles were bound too.

"They led you to believe that they were going away to help her, and that he was the only one that could find Tori." The voice continued on as if I hadn't even spoken.

"How do you know about Tori?" I lifted my head off the cold stone ground, squinting through the darkness.

"They never planned on coming back, of course." The man ignored my query entirely.

I coughed the dust from my lungs, "you're lying."

"I wish I was…for your sake," he mumbled. "Your best friend and your girlfriend taking off together…"

I followed the outline of the person pacing in front of me. The bulky figure stood tall, almost the height of the ceiling that was slowly coming into vision.

Trixie would never do such a thing, of course. The

way she looked at me, the way she held me—there was no way. And Jake, he's been my best friend since we were teenagers. I had full trust in him. I knew this man trying to probe anger from me and I had to keep my head on straight. I would not let him manipulate me.

I swallowed, but said nothing.

"You must feel betrayed," the man went on, "she made you believe that you meant everything to her, just so she could stab you in the back and run off with your best friend."

Gritting my teeth, I stared ahead. It wasn't true. *Why was he trying to turn me against her? What was the purpose of it?*

"No? Nothing?" The man continued pacing the room for a moment, then stopped right in front of me. "Well, that's disappointing. I'll let you mole it over."

I watched his boots walk away from me to the door. He tapped on the door and a little window that I could just make out on it opened. The window closed, and the door opened to allow him to leave. I tried to peer outside the door, but it was just a dark corridor lined with candles.

The door slammed shut, and I slumped my head back on the cold stone floor.

HOURS OR DAYS had gone by—I wasn't sure how long. Someone would come in and leave a tray of bread and water, and I would be taken down the hall every so often to relieve myself before being thrown back into this room.

No one had spoken to me since that first day. I asked questions, but only silence or grunts followed.

Wherever Jake and Trixie were, I hoped they were safe, and that she was getting the help from Tori that she needed. *Had they even found Tori?* I could only hope they had.

What I hadn't worked out yet was what they wanted from me. *Why had they captured me?* There was nothing I could give them. They had already stolen everything from me. *What more did they want?*

Eleven

TRIXIE

TRAINING HAD STARTED. Days had passed. Tori kept to herself, except during my sessions. She only spoke to give me instructions.

Jake tagged along at the sessions, but kept his distance. He watched from afar.

"Magic needs to be used." Tori explained during one session. "Not using it is causing it to be trapped in your soul. It's aching to come out, so it's forcing the magic to happen when you lose control emotionally."

I nodded. "That makes sense."

"So, using it every day will give the magic the release it needs." Tori said. "It will stop emerging when you don't want it to. You'll gain control of it when it releases."

I nodded again.

"Alright, try again," she said.

Taking a deep breath, I stared at the tree in front of me. Focusing on the low branches, I imagined the branches growing larger. At first, nothing happened. Then the bark moved as the wood expanded. The leaves rustled, and the tree creaked as the branches continued to grow another metre.

"Good. You're getting better," Tori stated. "Now, control the release."

I halted the branches' growth. Focusing ahead, I imagined the tree the way it had been. Slowly, the bark shifted and sunk back into the tree and it went back to normal.

"Well done," Tori said, walking past me. "That's enough for today."

"Thank you." I smiled and looked over at Jake.

He pushed himself off his chosen boulder, and we silently followed Tori back toward her hidden home.

TORI AND I sat in her makeshift lounge room while Jake washed up after dinner. I fiddled with my sleeve, trying to ignore the growing tension.

"You and Jake seem close." Tori broke the silence.

My fingers froze on the material; I released my clothing and nodded. "He's a good friend."

"Just friends?"

I frowned. "Yes, of course."

Tori nodded.

We sat in silence for a long while. She bounced her knee and tapped the armrest with her long, delicate fingers.

"I'm ashamed that I hurt him," she said, a sadness in her shaky voice. "I thought so much about how I didn't want to hurt him. I ended up doing exactly that."

I swallowed and shifted in the chair, crossing my ankles.

"The fact that you don't have control over it, yet the other day you somehow managed to keep him safe from it…" she shook her head. "I envy you."

"What?" I let out an awkward laugh.

"It's true," Tori whispered. "I'm jealous."

"Don't be. There's nothing to be jealous about."

"Yes, there is," she said. "You're stronger than you think you are. And I think you're a stronger Elemental than me."

"No way. I can't control it, you can."

"That doesn't mean I'm stronger. It only means I have control, not strength." Tori said.

I opened my mouth to speak, but closed it again. I listened to the clang of dishes in the kitchen. *Could Jake hear us?*

"He's been looking for you for years, you know." I said.

Tori stared ahead.

"He and Kieran have been searching villages to try find you." I explained. "Now that he's found you, he doesn't know how to tell you he still loves you."

Tori snapped her eyes to mine and glanced away.

"That's history," she said. "We aren't together anymore."

I watched her for a moment. "You still love him, too."

She closed her eyes, a deep sadness etched across her face.

"It's not too late, Tori." I whispered. "He wants you to come home with us."

"I-I can't." Her voice shook, and she opened her eyes. "I almost killed him. I can't put him in that danger again."

"You have control now. You would save him. He's miserable without you."

She shook her head and stood up. "I'm tired."

"Tori—."

"Sorry, I need to get some sleep." She moved toward the hallway without looking at me. "You need your sleep too."

I sighed, and she left me alone in the lounge room. Exhaustion seeping through my bones, but my mind was wide awake.

MY VISION BLURRED, and everything around me changed. The beautiful snow capped trees melted away to stone. The fresh snow beneath my feet turned into a hard stone floor and the refreshing cool air turned damp and humid. I wrinkled my nose as the stench of mould reached my nostrils.

Flecks of snow fell to the stone ground. I frowned at the oddity of it. A cool breeze touched my cheek, and a shiver ran down my spine. *What happened?* Tori and Jake were gone. The eerie corridor I stood in was familiar. Too familiar. My dreams. This was the corridor that kept haunting me.

My heart pounded in my chest and I stepped forward. I didn't move far. My eyes blurred again, and I froze in place. The corridor warped into a room. I swallowed as my vision cleared and a shirtless man stood in the middle of the space facing sideways to me. My breath caught as I stared at the too familiar muscles of his arms and stomach.

The stray strand of hair that usually fell down over his face was absent. His head hung forward, all his hair falling over his face. I followed the line of his arms up to the brass chains holding his wrists together above him.

I scanned his body and paused on his legs, which hung at odd angles. His pants had torn, and dirt and blood covered his skin.

Blood.

I tried to swallow the lump forming in my throat with

no success. My eyes snapped to the gashed on his back. Some are shallow and some deep. The shallow cuts had dried blood on them, but the deeper ones were still wet. My hands shook, and I reached toward him. My feet wouldn't move forward.

The snow fell heavier around me, building a thin layer on the stone floor and in my hair. I stared with wide eyes at Kieran's unmoving body. Watching his chest, I released a breath when I saw the rise and fall.

"Kieran?" I whispered, the word barely leaving my lips.

He didn't move. The snow blurred my vision, and the stone transformed back into bark. I blinked.

"Trixie?" Tori's voice sounded beside me.

I collapsed onto my hands and knees in the cold.

"Trixie, what happened?" Tori's hand rested on my shoulder and she knelt beside me.

Weeping, I covered my face with my hands. My knees dug into the fresh snow, only vaguely aware of Jake standing nearby. A dream while awake was bizarre, and this was the worst one yet. The lacerations on his back...so deep.

"Please, tell us what happened," Tori said. "Your—your eyes were solid white, and you looked horrified."

The pounding in my chest threatened to leap out of my ribs. My mind burst with emotion—tears streaked down my cheek.

Tori shifted beside me. "Trixie?"

"Kieran—," I choked, dropping my hands. "He was chained up. H-he was hurt."

Jake crouched in front of me, a hand on my shoulder. "What do you mean?"

"Uh…" my eyes met Jake's.

"What exactly did you see?" Tori asked.

"A stone corridor and a stone room. Like the ones I often dream about." My brows pulled in and I looked at Tori. "He had cuts on his back. Some were still bleeding."

"Was he…?" Jake started.

"He was still breathing." I looked between my two companions. Snow was thick on their clothes and hair. "It snowed."

"Yes, it snows here." Tori raised her eyebrows.

I shook my head. "No, I mean, in my dream. It was snowing *inside*."

Tori exchanged a quick glance with Jake.

"You weren't dreaming." Tori bit her lip.

"What?" I said.

"Your dreams aren't dreams. They are visions."

My mouth opened slightly, and my lip quivered. Jake stared at Tori, as dumbfounded as I was.

"Visions?" I whispered. "But, that means…"

"He really is hurt." Jake said.

Tori glanced at Jake. "Yes."

"But where is he?" I asked, wiping the wetness away with the back of my hand.

"What else did you see? Any windows?" Tori asked.

I shook my head. "No windows. It was just stone walls, floors, roof. It was damp and humid. I don't think it was a cave…maybe a building?"

"Come on." Tori stood. "Let's get back and prepare to leave."

I blinked and looked up at her. "Where are we going?"

"Myrdreya." Tori said. "We have to confirm he's really missing first. Then, we find him."

My stomach lurched. If Tori was right, Kieran was in danger and we had to find him. *What if the visions weren't real? What if they were? What if we were too late?*

⁂

HOURS LATER, WE arrived on the floating platform at Myrdreya. It was empty. We stared out into the city and only saw a couple of people wandering. It was too quiet. My body tensed. I scanned over the few people nearby—but they acted like they normally would.

"Where is everyone?" I asked.

"I was wondering the same thing." Tori said.

Jake strode forward. "Come on, let's find Demetri."

"Wait." Tori said. "We need to check that Kieran really isn't here first."

"Right." Jake said.

Nodding, I said, "I'll check our room."

"Let's check the training room." Jake said to Tori. "Trixie, meet us in front of the mansion in ten minutes."

I nodded and hurried to my room. I bolted down the hall, passing two Soul Weavers along the way. They jumped out of my way, frowning as I passed.

My hand pushed on the door and I stared inside. The room was empty. My eyes gazed over the room and settled on a note sitting on the perfectly made bed. I hurried over and scrambled to open it.

We have Kieran.

My heart stopped, and I stared at the roughly scrawled words. I flipped the note over to find more, but those 3 words were all that was written. A tear seeped down my cheek and I wiped it away.

I bolted from the room, paper in hand. Not bothering to close the door, I hurried back down the hall, passing the same Soul Weavers I had almost bouldered over the first time. I mumbled a quick apology and exited the mansion.

"THEY HAVE HIM" I shouted, holding up the note as Tori and Jake came into view.

"Who?" Jake strode over to me, grasping the note from my hand.

"I-I don't know." I stuttered.

Jake looked up from the paper. "We will find him. I promise you."

"Let's get to Demetri," Tori said. "Work out a plan."

Twelve

KIERAN

THE MANACLES AROUND MY WRISTS ached. Bruises and blisters wilted. They stopped any kind of magic, otherwise I would have already escaped this wretched place.

Planting my feet on the ground, my legs trembling, I stood, releasing the pressure on my hands. My back stung; the cuts I knew were surely deep from the metal stick I was beaten with hours earlier.

The fire lantern on the wall flickered, the embers low. The lock on the metal door slid, and it creaked open.

"Ah...you're finally awake."

A chill swept down my spine. That female's voice was familiar, yet it couldn't be. Turning my head toward her, I stared at the young Soul Weaver before me. I blinked and frowned.

"Shocked to see me?" she said. "It's like seeing a ghost, isn't it?"

My chest rose and dropped. I swallowed as I stared at Sienna.

"How is it possible? We saw you die..." my voice trailed off.

She pursed her lips. "Did you though?"

"I don't understand."

"Let me enlighten you." Her mouth curved at the corner and walked around to stand in front of me. "I never killed my parents. I was always in control of my powers and never needed saving."

She encircled me. My mind whirled. I followed her movement with my eyes, turning in my cuffs to keep her in my sight.

"It was all fake. We drew you to me so I could see my sister. The plan was ruined when so many of you came to..." she altered her voice to sarcasm. "*Rescue poor Sienna from losing control.*"

"Your sister?"

She stopped pacing, and a wicked grin crossed her face. "Trixie."

My breathing accelerated, and my palms sweated.

"She had a brother, not a sister." I breathed.

"Aw, they really like lying to you, don't they?" Sienna said, not expecting an answer. She continued. "They couldn't have anyone piecing it together that she had a sister, or I would have been hunted down along with Trixie. So Trixie was the bait, and I was left alone gathering followers."

I shook my head. "Followers?"

"Dark Soul Weavers." Sienna clarified.

"There was no son?" I muttered.

Sienna smiled. "No. He was made up."

"But, Jay, he is on our side and he knew about the son."

"See, this is the exciting part," she said, pacing the room again. "Dad pretended to be on Trixie's side, to love her and help you remove my Mother from Myrdreya. When *really* he was acting as a spy, staying in the city to find weaknesses. He discovered how close you and Trixie were that he knew it would be the perfect way to draw you both out of the city."

I stared at her, dumbfounded. I couldn't believe what I was hearing. Jay was on Julianne's side all this time. He faked his love for Trixie. Faked his loyalty to Myrdreya. He faked his apology to me.

I shook my head again. "No, it doesn't make sense. We broke the spell on Jay. Julianne was controlling him."

Sienna's wicked smile broadened. "He was never being controlled. Well, not entirely anyway. Julianne placed a controlling spell on him that only partially controlled him, just enough to make his eyes glassy. Other than that, he was doing everything on his own."

My eyes dropped to the floor. Devastation inched along my skin, soaking my blood and heart. Not for me though, for Trixie. She would be distraught.

"Heart breaking, isn't it?" Sienna said, and she clapped her hands together. "I can't wait to see Trixie's face when she finds out!"

"Stay away from her." I said through gritted teeth.

Sienna tilted her head. "I'm willing to bet that she's already looking for you. So, I won't need to stay away from her. She will come."

"No." I twisted in my shackles, my wrists searing with pain. " I won't let you."

She laughed. "And how do you expect to save her?"

A groan erupted from my throat. "What do you want with her?"

"Ah…" she sighed. "You will have to wait and see."

Thirteen

BANG. Bang. Bang.

I slammed my fist into the glass door. "DEMETRI!"

An outline appeared, and the door clicked open. Demetri's green eyes looked us up and down.

"What's wrong?" he said, his eyes lingering on Tori. "Tori, this is a…pleasant surprise."

Jake shifted beside me, drawing my attention to him. His shoulders tensed and his jaw clenched.

"It's been a long time, Demetri." Tori said. "But we'll

have to save the pleasantries for later."

"Kieran is missing." Jake blurted.

Demetri pursed his lips and turned away. I glanced at Jake, frowning. He followed Demetri into the room. Tori and I lingered just inside the doorway.

"You knew he was missing." Jake accused.

Demetri turned, his jaw shifted as he gritted his teeth and eyed Jake. "He's been missing for days."

"Days?" I breathed, my chest tightened.

"Who has him?" Tori asked.

Demetri sighed. "I've got an address you should go check out."

Demetri moved to his desk and scrawled on a small piece of paper.

"I think you will find answers here," he said, handing me the note.

I swallowed, staring at the address. I didn't recognise it. Tori and Jake leaned over and looked at it.

"Let's go." I said and started out the door.

"Wait." Jake said, staring at Demetri. "So, you don't know who took him?"

Demetri looked over our faces. He appeared to be hesitating on how to answer Jake's question.

"I think you know who," he said.

Jake nodded and left the room. Tori and I trailed after Jake, down the spiralling ramp.

"My mother, right?" I said.

Jake said nothing for a long moment. Tori glanced at

me and settled her eyes on Jake.

"We need to find Clara." He said.

WE FOUND CLARA about to enter the training grounds. She immediately bounded over when she saw us and threw her arms around Tori.

"So good to see you!" Clara said, and she released Tori, grinning.

"Do you know about Kieran?" Jake said, and the smile wiped clean off Clara's face.

Clara swallowed, eyeing of us. "What do you mean?"

"He's been taken." I said, and Clara's eyes locked on mine.

"What?" Clara shook her head. "No, he went on a secret mission for Demetri days ago."

"Demetri didn't tell you…" Jake's voice trailed.

Clara shifted on her feet. "Tell me what?"

"Demetri has known for days that he went missing. We went to see him and…he's hiding something."

"I had a feeling as well." Tori said. "He seemed to avoid a direct answer."

Jake stepped forward. "I could feel he was lying. He was trying to get around my question, but…"

Clara stalked past us. Jake tore after her, and Tori and I glanced at each other before following.

We followed Clara up the spiralling ramp. She barged straight into the room without knocking.

"Demetri?" Clara called out.

We entered the room and looked around. Demetri wasn't at his desk and his bedroom door was ajar. Jake crossed the room and peered around the frame.

"He's not here." Jake said.

"Maybe he's gone for dinner?" Tori suggested, but her voice sounded unsure.

I glanced at Clara. Her eyes were far away. I watched her, narrowing my eyes. *Was she using her senses?*

"He's not in Myrdreya." Clara stated.

Tori and Jake stared at her.

"We just spoke to him only five minutes ago." I said.

"Let's ask the portal keeper where he went." Clara said, stalking out of the room.

"There's something we should tell you." I said, my eyes on Clara.

Clara hesitated outside the room, but said nothing. I filled Clara in on my dreams—no, my visions—particularly the latest one, as we hurried through the city to the portal room.

"Are you sure the visions are real?" Clara asked.

I nodded. "They felt so real."

"They're real." Tori said. "I've done my fair share of research on visions, and hers are definitely real."

"Right." Clara said, biting her lip. "In that case, let's hurry."

We reached the portal room minutes later.

"Mae, where did Demetri port to?" Jake asked.

Mae stared at him and glanced at us before answering.

"Um…I'm not supposed to tell anyone."

"Demetri is a traitor." Jake stated, and Mae's eyes widened.

"Please, Mae," I begged, "Kieran's in trouble."

"The woods east of Plymort, west of the Igor Mountains."

"Do you know why he went there?" I asked.

Her eyes locked on mine. "No, but he seemed to be in a hurry."

"Of course he was." Jake mumbled. "Mae, please open a new portal to Igor Mountains—where you had just ported him."

"Certainly." Mae reached her hand out in front of her.

MY FEET LANDED in dense undergrowth. Small animals scurried away, hiding in nearby shrubbery. Between the gaps in the trunks, I could make out the small town of Plymort. Clara and Tori were standing a short way to the left of me, and Jake's boots sounded to the right. I glanced over at Jake, his eyes fixated on the trees surrounding us.

"It's only been, what…8 minutes since he would have ported?" Tori said, eyeing the trees to the left of us.

"He can't have gotten far?" I questioned, turning

around to gaze into the forest behind us.

"It's been long enough..." Jake muttered, but he stopped talking and his face went blank.

I knew the look of someone pushing out their senses now. It was easy to see when you knew what you were looking at—the blank expression; the eyes staring far off into the distance or closed. I glanced at Clara; she stared off to the right with the same blank expression.

"Nothing." Clara said in almost a whisper.

Tori shook her head. "Where would he have gone?"

"He's clever." Jake said, blinking and his eyes settling on me. "He's gone."

"What?" I breathed, my heart hammering.

"He ported here and then must have taken another portal to somewhere else so we couldn't trace him." He said.

"What do we do now?" Clara said.

"How do we find him?" I said, looking into the trees.

We were all silent for a long time. The wind rustled the leaves, and the branches creaked. Tears leaked from my eyes, my lips quivering.

"Let's start at the address he gave us," Tori said, my blurry eyes came to rest on her.

"It's probably a deterrence." Jake said, pacing.

"Probably." Clara said. "But it's all we have."

I gulped.

They weren't giving up—and neither was I.

WE STEPPED THROUGH Mae's portal and stood in a dark street. A chill ran along my spine as I stared down the empty road. Cars were parked on the side of the bitumen, here and there. Only one street lamp was halfway down, and all lights in the buildings were off—except for one. A dull blue light emitted from a window a few buildings down.

"Number 49," Clara whispered, clearly not wanting to attract unwanted attention.

Jake stepped forward, peering toward the closest building for a number. The walls were brown and rusting, windows cracked. My heart pounded in my chest, the hairs on the back of my neck stood on end. I brushed my hands over my arms, though I wasn't cold.

"44," Jake said and thrusted his chin forward to show for us to continue down the gloomy street.

The paint on the dilapidated buildings peeled and chipped, revealing crumbling brick and rusted metal. We walked past boarded-up windows and cracked sidewalks, the only signs of life being a stray cat curled up in an abandoned doorway. In front of one house, a metal gate stood ajar, the lock broken and ivy vines overgrown on the gate and fences. I could see the soft glow of the blue light beyond the fence.

Tori pointed at the gate and we all followed her gaze to the digits nailed on it.

"49," I whispered, my breath barely escaping my trembling lips.

"Stay together. Look for any signs of Kieran or danger." Jake whispered. "If we get split up, stay in pairs."

Tori stepped forward, squeezing through the gap of the gate opening. Clara followed her. Jake nodded to me and I stepped through the gate. I turned back to check, he followed behind me.

We scanned the outside of the building. It appeared to be vacant, but the light told us otherwise. It was an old brick and wood house—or a store; I wasn't entirely sure. The grey paint was peeling on the front double doors and the windows were large but covered mostly by curtains except for the blue light seeping out between the curtains.

Tori tried the door handle, and it opened with a soft click. Tori and Jake glanced at one another for a split second before she pushed the door open. A short hallway met us beyond the threshold, a doorway on the left and another on the right.

Jake indicated for Clara and Tori to go left and Jake and I to go right. He obviously didn't want me out of his sight. *Who could blame him?* He promised Kieran he would look after me, so that was exactly what he was going to do.

Jake and I stepped through the doorway on the right, toward the glow of the strange light. *Why would anyone have a blue light on? What was it coming from?*

Keeping close together, I followed Jake into the room. It was only a small room, and it was empty except for a recliner chair by the window. A door stood ajar on the left, from it was the blue light flowing into the room.

Jake held up his hand before he stepped around the corner. He froze, his face glowing blue. His eyes scanned the room, but he didn't move.

"Jake?" I whispered from beside him.

He moaned but didn't move his lips.

"What's wrong?" I stepped closer.

An angry groan emitted from his throat—or maybe a growl—I wasn't sure. I halted and stared over at his unmoving posture.

The blood drained from my face, and I suddenly felt a cold chill down my spine. *Oh, fuck.* He couldn't move his limbs. The beating behind my rib cage threatened to jump out of my body. My palms clammy and my knees weak, my muscles trembled.

I stepped forward and reached out to touch Jake on the arm. Before I could touch him, someone knocked my feet out from under me and I fell face-first onto the mouldy, dusty floorboards.

I groaned at the sudden fall, my hands reaching to feel my nose. Wet and sticky. Blood. *Great.* I groaned again. It didn't feel broken, thankfully. *But what made me fall?* I pushed myself up to my knees, turning my head to gaze up at Jake.

A blow to my stomach had me gagging and falling to the ground again. *What the?* I rolled to the side and stared up at a shadowed figure standing over me. The blue light faintly lit up their face, enough for me to see them. A smirk curled on the woman's lips as she stared down at me.

"Welcome home...sis."

Fourteen

THE SMELL OF MOULD AND dust reached my nostrils as I stirred awake. *What happened?* My hand reached up to my head; it throbbed. Knocked out again. *Super.*

"I was beginning to wonder if you were ever going to wake." A familiar voice reached my ears.

Pushing myself off the dirty ground, I gazed around in the darkness. I knew that voice, but it sounded huskier than usual.

Blinking away the black, my vision cleared enough to

see an outline of a person sitting against a wall to my right. Seating myself against the nearest wall, I lifted a hand to my nose. The stickiness was gone.

"I...erm...cleaned you up when they threw you in here."

I swallowed. *Yes, it was definitely him.* Levi.

"Thank you." I croaked, dropping my hand.

"Are you hurt anywhere else?" he asked.

I shook my head. "No."

Staring ahead for a long silent moment, I watched as the room we were in came into view as my eyes adjusted. A dull light streamed down from high in the ceiling. *A sunlight?* The walls were brick and thick with mould. I wrinkled my nose.

"You'll get used to the smell." Levi mumbled, his head leaning back and resting on the brick wall.

"Where are we?" I eyed him. "Why are you here?"

He shrugged. "I don't know where we are."

He paused and shifted his bare feet, crossing his ankles and leaning his elbows on his knees. His hands cupped together, chin resting on them. I waited for him to continue.

"As for why I'm here..." he hesitated only a second before continuing. "I overheard the Soul Hunters talking about kidnapping you."

"So, explain to me why you were at Sienna's house." I glared at him, crossing my arms. "Are you still working with the Soul Hunters? Was everything you said a lie?"

He shook his head, dropping his hands from his face. "No, I never lied to you."

"Then why were you there?"

"It's not what it seemed…" he started.

I raised my eyebrows, crossing my arms.

"I was spying on the Soul Hunters. I found them going to that house." He sighed. "I climbed the grate to the second floor and hid in the stairwell. While trying to listen to them, I heard your whispers, so I retreated to the room."

"You knew I came?"

"No, I didn't know it was you until Kieran and you appeared at the door." Levi said.

"So, you were following them because they were going to kidnap me?" I asked.

"Yes," he nodded. "And when you turned up I knew they must have been trying to get both of you."

"Both of us?" I frowned.

"Sienna is your sister." Levi stated.

I shook my head. "She called me sis before she knocked me out. I don't understand. I have a brother—not a sister."

"He was a lie." Levi's eyes saddened.

"No," I shook my head. "You're lying."

"I wish I was." He sighed. "You never had a brother. Your parents hid Sienna so no one would find out she existed until they needed her to show herself."

"What? That can't be true…that w-would m-mean…"

my voice broke and trailed off.

"I'm sorry, but it's true." Levi said, scrubbing his hand down his face. "Your father is…"

"Don't say it!" I blurted out, shoving my hands against the wall to push myself up to stand.

Levi fell silent. I paced the small brick room we were trapped in, eyeing the door as I stalked past. The black door was bolted.

I pointed at the door. "I assume that's magic protected?"

Levi nodded.

I pursed my lips and continued pacing. "Why didn't you stop us going downstairs to save Sienna? How did she even survive?"

"I didn't know what Sienna was capable of. I'm sorry, I shouldn't have let you go down there." Levi stared at the dirty ground, avoiding my gaze. "Two Soul Hunters, an out of control Soul Weaver, should have been easy for the 4 of you."

I stopped pacing and stared at the top of his head. He still avoided looking at me. *Had he just insulted us?*

"If I had known how powerful she was…" he shook his head. "I promise you, I wouldn't have let you go down there. I would have warned you."

I gritted my teeth; he hadn't answered my second question.

"She lost control and killed the two Soul Hunters." I spat.

"I don't think she lost control." He muttered. "She burned them, thinking she would kill you all as well. How did you survive?"

"How did *she* survive?" I growled as I paced again.

"I don't know." Levi shook his head, his eyes lifted to mine. "But I'm glad you did. I was so worried you hadn't. By the time I came downstairs, the room was burnt and everyone was gone."

I huffed and leant against the opposite wall from him, adverting my eyes to the dull light above.

"Trix, I'm sorry about your family." He said.

"How did you get in here?" I said, redirecting the conversation onto him.

"Well, after I left Sienna's house, I was making my way back and…" he shrugged. "I was ambushed by Soul Hunters and locked up here. Been here ever since."

"How did they catch you?" I asked, staring directly at him.

He shifted his legs and stood. "I was pretending to still be on their side, told them I had been on a secret mission for Julianne the day we attacked the city."

I frowned. "Why would you do that?"

"When I found out they were planning to kidnap you, I wanted to be in the loop so I could help you escape…" he sighed and leaning his head back on the wall. "But, I was caught out. Julianne found out, and I was put in here."

"That was really stupid. She could have killed you."

I raised my eyebrows. "What happened to seeking a normal life?"

"I was going to…but I couldn't stop thinking about Julianne getting away from the city. Demetri just let her go. I don't get it. Why would he do that?" Levi's forehead creased.

"Because Demetri is a traitor." I said.

"What?"

"He's on her side." I swallowed. "He had Kieran captured, I know it."

"Kieran's been captured too?"

I nodded. "I just don't know where. You haven't seen him, have you?"

Levi shook his head. "No. I haven't seen much of this place. Why do you think Demetri is a traitor?"

"We asked him about Kieran and he was avoiding our questions. Then, he left the city in a hurry. We tried to follow him, but he was gone." I said, sliding down the wall onto my bottom.

Levi stepped forward and started toward me. I watched him from the corner of my eye as he seated himself next to me. I rested my head against the cold bricks. It was slightly comforting having Levi locked in the same cell as me; I was able to get some answers, and I had someone to talk to. Better than being alone.

My eyes drooped. Exhaustion riddled my bones. Pictures of the metal gate with ivy vines and the blue light swam into my mind. I snapped my eyes open wide.

"JAKE!" I yelled.

"No, just Levi." Levi said next to me.

I shook my head. "No, Jake was there with me when Sienna came. And, Clara and Tori were in the building too. Do you know if…?"

Levi's blank expression said it all. He hadn't seen them.

"They didn't come here with me?" I asked.

"I don't think so. I was in the hallway being escorted back here when they brought you in. You were alone."

I let a whoosh of air out of my lungs. "They must have gotten away…"

Jake had been petrified. As soon as that blue light had touched him, he couldn't move. I shivered.

"Do you know much about Sienna's powers?" I asked.

"Not really." He replied. "I haven't really seen her."

I nodded, leaning my head back against the bricks. I closed my eyes, knowing I couldn't do much while exhausted, anyway. Allowing myself to drift off to sleep, I slumped sideways, vaguely aware of my head resting on something boney, but warm.

I BEGAN STIRRING, a mouldy and dusty stench wafting up my nostrils. Shifting my head, a bone dug into my ear and a new warmth rested around me. I snapped my eyes open. Bare feet, legs covered in jeans, and a black shirt.

I bolted upright; the warmth falling away from me. Levi and I stared at one another for a moment before I tore my eyes away from him. His arm rested limply beside me. It had been around me. I had been lying on his shoulder. *Oh, god.*

I cleared my throat. "Sorry."

"It's fine." Levi said, stretching and pulling his arm back to his lap. "It was warmer than it has been, so it was nice."

I glanced over at the door. Two food trays had been left there.

"When did those arrive?" I asked.

"Only about 10 minutes ago."

I eyed the dull silver trays; bread and water. *Awesome.*

"That's all they've been feeding you?" I asked, turning my head back to him.

"Mostly." He sighed. "Sometimes I get left over soup, or a half-eaten sandwich."

"Great…" I rolled my eyes.

"Better than nothing, though, right?" He said, standing to stretch out his legs.

"I guess." I murmured.

Clanking outside the door shot our attention to it. I jumped to my feet, and we stared as the door pushed open. A woman with red hair and brown eyes waltzed in.

"Good, you're awake. Otherwise, I would have been kicking you awake." A smirk spread across her face.

Delaras. I glared at my former neighbour. She glanced

down at our food trays and lifted a brow.

"Bread wasn't good enough for you?" She chuckled. "No matter, you'll soon be begging for it."

"What do you want?" Levi growled.

Delaras turned her eyes on Levi. "You will respect your elders, boy."

Levi spat at her feet. Delaras' nostrils flared, but she said nothing. She watched Levi for a moment longer before turning back to me.

"She wants to see you," Delaras said.

"My mother or my imaginary sister?" I said sarcastically, rolling my eyes..

Delaras' lip curled at the corner and she tilted her head. "You look a lot like your older sister. Pity you couldn't have complied along with her."

"I have no sister." I said through gritted teeth.

"Believe what you want." She said. "But she's waiting to see you."

Delaras stepped aside, indicating with her hand for me to exit the cell. I glanced at Levi. He stood with his fists clenched. Tension radiated from his body.

"Oh, don't worry, you'll be back with Levi soon." Delaras taunted. "Although I had thought I might have found you strangled him for being a traitor."

"You're the traitor."

"Aren't we all?" Delaras stepped out into the hall.

Taking a breath, I tore my eyes from Levi and followed Delaras out into the hall. The cell door banged shut behind us, followed by the lock hitting home.

Our footsteps echoed off the empty hallway, the stone quickly turning to dirt. The sound of my breathing, loud in my ears. The coldness of the damp air seeping into bones, bringing back the memories of my mind not being my own. I shivered, and it had nothing to do with the cold.

We turned left, traveling in silence along another vacant hallway. A man stood halfway down, eyeing us as we approached. Dressed in black and red like Delaras, he smirked, stepping aside so we could enter the doorway he guarded.

Vanilla, caramel and musk reached my nostrils—a pleasant aroma compared to the mouldy cave. Entering the room, an empty grey table with two chairs sat in the centre. My eyes were drawn to the figure I despised—Sienna. She stood in the corner, her arms crossed, her expression blank.

Delaras pushed me toward the table and pressed my shoulders down, forcing me to sit in a chair. She didn't wait for dismissal. Her footsteps faded as she left. I twisted in the uncomfortable plastic chair. The guard stood back in the entry, his back facing us.

"It's good to see you, sis." Sienna's melodramatic voice stung in my ears and I turned to face her.

"Save the pleasantries, sis—*ter*." I spat the last syllable.

Sienna sighed, uncrossing her arms and rolling her

shoulders. "It's uncomfortable sleeping in a cave, is it?"

"Like you would know."

"Oh," she giggled. "That's right...you would be even more uncomfortable with no bed at all."

I rolled my eyes. "What do you want with me?"

She pouted. "Well, you see...you have something we want."

"We? Oh, you mean you and your parents?" I crossed my arms.

"*Our* parents."

Ignoring her correction, I said, "so, where are they anyway?"

"Not here."

"Oh damn, I thought they were hiding under the table." Sarcasm rolling off my tongue.

She pushed off the wall. "You're one piece of the puzzle, and when we find the other, you will give me what I want."

"What *you* want? A moment ago, it was what *we* want." I raised my eyebrows.

She stared at me, her eyes flickering between mine. *Good, I pressed a button.* Two can play that game.

"So, what is this other piece? Your heart?"

Sienna's eyes narrowed, and her jaw ticked.

"I personally don't think it can be found. Just like your parents, you've got no heart."

She slammed her hand on the desk. I jolted backward, uncrossing my arms and holding onto the edge of the seat. Her fingers turned molten, and the desktop blackened where they touched.

"I have power beyond your imagination." She hissed.

"Where is Kieran?" I demanded, my eyes switching focus between her hands and her blue eyes—*my* blue eyes.

Sienna pursed her lips. "Oh, he's…somewhere."

"Don't touch him, or I'll—."

"You'll what?" She spat, her face closer to mine. "*Slow me?*"

My eyes widened, and I frowned. *How would she know about my gift?*

"That's right. I know about your little gift." She smirked and leaned back. "I know you used it when your friend was killed and you were surprised. If only you had worked out, you could slow time *before* he snapped her neck."

Blood drained from my face. Bile rose in my throat. Kiarra's horrified face swam at the front of my memories. Her terrified eyes begging me to help her—but I could do nothing but stand there. The crack of her neck snapping and her lifeless body falling to the floor sent shivers down my spine. My heart broke into pieces all over again.

Sienna was right. If I had known, I could have saved her. Kiarra could have been safe in Myrdreya with me. Guilt gripped my heart and squeezed.

"Ah…I hit a nerve, huh?"

I clenched my jaw, staring at the wall ahead. I fixated on the mouldy stone, breathing slowly and balling my hands into fists. The stone shuddered, and I focused every thought on the wall to keep it from warping.

"Well?" Sienna huffed.

The stone stilled, and I released my fists; my palms stung from where my nails had pierced the skin.

"Was that the first time you used it?" Sienna asked, her voice distant as I ignored her.

I was done. Done with talking to her.

Sienna continued speaking, but I shut her out, not hearing another word. She eventually sighed and flicked her hand. A moment later, the guard gripped my arms, hauling me to my feet and led me back down the hallway. His strong fingers wrapped around my upper arm; I'll probably have bruises later. My feet dragged along the stone floor, my shoulders slumped. I wasn't sure how long we had been walking; I paid no mind to the travel back to the cell.

When the door slammed shut behind me, Levi was hunched in the cell's corner. He sprang to his feet as the lock clicked. His arms were around me before I could speak.

"Are you okay?" His voice whispered in my ear. "I was worried you wouldn't come back."

"I'm okay." I said, my arms hanging by my sides.

Levi released me and stepped back. "Sorry."

I shook my head. "It's fine."

"What did she want?" His hand lightly ran along my forearm.

"To talk."

Levi tilted his head. "About…"

I turned away from him, biting my lip. Not sure how much I should tell him yet, I said, "She was just boasting about her powers."

"Was that all?"

I turned back to face him. "And she wants something from me."

"What?" He frowned.

"She didn't say." I pulled at my fingers. "Don't worry about it."

Levi stepped toward me. "I won't let her hurt you."

He reached up to my face, tucking a strand behind my ear. I watched him, trying to read his thoughts. He leaned toward me, his lips parting slightly. I jolted backwards, holding my hands up.

"Wow," was all that escaped my mouth.

"S-sorry…old habits." Levi shook his head and looked away.

I swallowed, walking over to the wall and leaning my shoulder against the cold, mouldy brick.

"I—." I began, but the room melted away.

I stared ahead at the bricks warping and moving. This wasn't me. I wasn't warping them. I frowned as I stared at the new sight in front of me.

The room had changed into a much larger room with

a long table lined with chairs.

At first I thought there was no one here, but then a voice beside me made my stomach churn.

"They know." I stared at Demetri; his white hair looked out of place against the dark stone walls.

Julianne sighed. "I knew it would only be a matter of time. Did you send word to Jay?"

Demetri bowed his head. "Yes, my lady. He will arrive here soon."

She nodded. "Good. It won't be long and I'll have all my family back together again."

My heart pounded behind my ribs. The pulse heavy in my ears. My heart sank. Blood drained from my face. It was true. My father had been on her side all along. It had always been their plan. *But what did they want with me?*

"She's coming for Kieran. It will be hard to keep them apart." Demetri said.

Julianne smirked. "She will have to die before she sees him again."

My body convulsed. The room dissolved away, leaving me in the small, cold cell again. My knees buckled, and I collapsed.

Arms around me caught me from hitting the ground.

"Trix, what happened?" Levi's eyes were wide and staring into mine.

I allowed myself to lean on him, no longer being able to hold myself upright. My muscles shook and I couldn't catch my breath. Hyperventilating, I gripped onto his shirt.

"Kieran." I said between breaths. "I think—I think he's—I think they—."

Levi held onto me tighter. We slumped to the ground, and I curled against him, allowing him to comfort me.

"He's not dead." Levi stated.

"You didn't see—I saw—my vision." I said through sobs.

"Trix, he's not dead." He repeated. "Don't believe it until you really see it."

My entire body shook. *What if I never saw him again? What if I had to die to see him again because he's already gone?* My face was wet with tears and they soaked into Levi's shirt as I sobbed harder.

Levi placed a hand under my chin and lifted my face to his. We were so close that I could feel his breath on my face.

"You didn't tell me you had visions." His voice came out softly as he looked over my face.

"It's new—well, sort of." I breathed heavily to force myself to calm. "I would have dreams that would become real. But, I found out recently they aren't dreams at all. They are visions."

Levi wiped my cheeks. "What sort of visions?"

"Mostly of Kieran. Of bad things happening to him."

"You have real visions?" Levi whispered.

I nodded, shifting out of Levi's arms. "They took

Kieran and have been torturing him."

Levi's brows raised. "How do you know what you're seeing is real? It might not be."

"I just…" my eyes twitched, "I just know."

"Maybe it's all a trick? What if they are playing some mind game on you?"

"Can't be. They feel too real." I leant my head against the wall.

Closing my eyes, I hugged my knees. I refused to believe my visions weren't real. I hated Kieran getting hurt, but I feared it all being in my mind more.

Fifteen

TRIXIE

MANY TRAYS OF FOOD HAD come and gone. No more visits or summons. Sitting in the corner, leaning against the brick, I stared at the door. I ground my teeth and pulled at my fingers. *How many days had it been? How would we escape this hellhole and find Kieran?* I hadn't had any more visions of him—it made me nervous. *Was he still alive?*

Glancing over at Levi, he sat about a metre away, tapping a tune on his knees.

"What magic have they blocked?" I asked.

"Erm…" he stopped tapping.

"Sorry, I forget you're still new to the whole magic thing." I muttered. "So am I."

Levi watched me, his eyes trailing over my face.

"I've never actually asked you about your magic," he said, repositioning himself to face me.

"What do you want to know?" I asked, dropping my hands into my lap.

His eyes flicked away for a moment before he spoke. "Can you read minds?"

I laughed. "No."

He looked at me sheepishly. "Stupid question, huh?"

I considered his words. "No, not really. We all have…spell magic. We can use the magic to defend ourselves, blast people off their feet, paralyse them, repair broken things…"

"Can you heal?"

I shook my head. "No. But some of us have special gifts."

"Really?" Levi's brows raised. "Do you have a gift?"

I hesitated, shifting my legs to curl under me. "Yes, I do."

My mind trailed off, thinking about my visions. I didn't know anyone else that had real visions like me. *Was I the only one in the world?* No, I couldn't be. Tori knew the gift existed.

The *stasis* gift—as Kieran had called it—had caught me off guard. But it had also saved my life. Guilt strangled my heart again. *What if I had known about the stasis earlier?* I could have saved Kiarra's life, too.

What about my magic orbs connecting with Kierans? I hadn't thought about it before. *But was that a gift, too? How many gifts did I have?* Having one gift was special. *But, four? It must be unheard of, right?*

Warping—the first gift I had discovered, although I hadn't known it was real for years. My elemental gift, one of the rarest gifts known to Soul Weavers. Struggling to control it for many years, terrified of hurting someone.

If my parents hadn't abandoned me, if they had brought me to Myrdreya to train as a child...my life would have been entirely different. I would have met Kieran earlier. I would have met Tori earlier. She could have helped me control it years ago, and maybe I could have kept her strong in return. Maybe she would never have left Myrdreya, never left Jake.

I closed my eyes. I vaguely heard Levi ask me if I was okay while Tori's voice sounded in my head, "Breathe, think about what you want to do. Focus on it. Imagine it. Create it."

I snapped my eyes open, pouncing to my feet and facing the wall. "I'm going to try something. Stand close to me. I don't want to accidentally hurt you."

Levi's brows shot up his forehead, but he stood and stepped toward me.

"Magic won't work..." his voice trailed off.

"Stand behind me." I said, and he did so, regardless

of his obvious doubts. "You haven't seen what I can do, but don't freak out, okay?"

I looked over my shoulder at Levi. He was standing closer than I expected. I almost bumped straight into his face.

"What are you going to do?" he asked, his breath brushing my cheek.

"Warp the walls to get out of here." I glimpsed a flash of shock on Levi's face before I turned back toward the wall.

I pushed on my thoughts, seeing the bricks tumbling down and the room beyond emerging. I imagined a hallway leading us out into a forest. One by one, the stones vibrated and shifted, opening a hole in the cell wall.

I grinned and looked over my shoulder at Levi—his mouth hung open, eyes wide, as he gaped at the moving wall.

"Woah." He breathed.

"Let's go."

We bounded down the makeshift hall; the bricks moving out of our path as we went. Voices called behind us, drawing our attention to spin around. The yelling started when the cell door burst open and guards entered.

"What the?"

"How?"

"Get them!"

"Don't let her escape!"

I stared at the opening between us and them.

"Come on, let's go," Levi begged behind me.

Clearing my mind, I watched the men bolt toward us. I focused on them, ignoring Levi tugging on my arm.

"What...?" I heard Levi's voice beside me.

The guards moved slower than a sloth. Their expressions contorted with confusion and anger. I changed my focus on the hall opening and imagined it closing. The bricks didn't hesitate. They shifted one by one, closing the hole in the wall, the hallway closing up toward us. I glimpsed the guards through the gap before it closed. Their expressions had turned to shock and horror. We plunged into darkness.

Holding my hand up in front of me, I willed the magic to appear in my palm. An electric fireball formed in my hand, casting a turquoise light on our faces.

"Okay, when we get out of here, you have to explain what just happened." Levi muttered.

I nodded briefly and turned toward the hallway, away from the cell. Walking forward with my magic illuminating the way, I warped the bricks to continue weaving to an exit in a forest.

Something wet dripped from my nose. I reached my free hand up to wipe it away. Something dark glistened on the back of my hand. Blood. Levi didn't miss the movement.

"Are you okay?" he asked, peering over my shoulder.

"Mhmm."

I wiped the back of my hand on my shirt and continued walking through my makeshift tunnel. After a few minutes, the bricks merged with dirt and we were walking through a dirt tunnel. It began sloping upwards, stones, sticks and plant roots becoming visible.

"Since your magic works now," Levi cleared his throat. "Shouldn't we portal out of here?"

"No. We have to investigate where we are. Kieran might be in there. We need to know where to come back to."

"What if they move him before we can get back?"

"I have to take my chances. It's better than no lead at all." I said.

Drip. Drip. Drip.

Damn. The liquid dripped thickly from my nose. I wiped my nose again. *Just a bit further.* We were close to the surface — I had to release us into the forest.

Thicker roots appeared, and the dirt became damp. The smell of mould was far behind us. Only the scent of earth surrounded us as I continued warping our path to freedom. But, I grew weak. The blood nose was the telltale sign of that. My muscles were vibrating, my legs threatening to give way. I wouldn't be able to go much further.

Come on. I needed to get out of here. The air grew thick. Very little oxygen produced in the roots of the plants — and we were running out.

"How much further?" Levi asked, his breathing laboured.

"Roots are getting thicker. We must be close..." my voice trailed off as my knees buckled and I fell.

"Trix!"

Levi's arms swooped around me, stopping me from hitting the ground. The magic orb faded and disappeared, plunging us back into darkness.

"Trix? Are you okay?" Levi's voice shook.

"I'm okay," I sighed. "This much magic is..."

"It's weakening you." He finished.

I nodded, but remembering he couldn't see me, I said, "yes."

Levi placed my arm around his shoulders and pulled us upright again. I leaned my body weight on him.

"Are you able to create light again?" he asked.

Steadying myself against him, I lifted my free arm and asked for the magic to come back. The electricity licked fingers and formed a new orb of light.

Levi and I both stared around us.

"Um, Trix..."

From the release of my magic, the surrounding dirt had begun caving in on us. Roots snagged at our ankles. I looked down and saw one wrapping around my foot. We were being buried alive.

Fear coursed through my veins. Dirt showered on us as the earth enveloped us. I pushed against it.

Come on. Kieran is depending on me. We're almost there.

I squeezed my eyes shut.

His face swam in my vision; his beautiful sun-kissed skin and the strand of hair that refused to be tamed. But he wasn't smiling. Blood and dirt covered his body. His pain-stricken expression boring into my soul.

"Trix, we're running out of time." Levi said loudly in my ear.

My arm still tight around him, he supported my weight as I leaned heavily on his shoulder. Opening my eyes, I looked around us. *Shit.* The roots and dirt enclosed around our bodies. Levi's other shoulder was buried in the dirt and our legs were nowhere to be seen.

I pulled my hand closer, the orb so close to my face, the light illuminated our faces as fear raked our expressions. Breathing became heavy.

"Trix—."

"I know!" I yelped.

Roots entangled around my torso and wrist. The earth enfolding us. Levi gasped beside me. Roots gripped his throat and dirt half covered his face. *No!* The magic vanished from my palm, plunging us into darkness again.

We couldn't die. Not like this. Not now. I had to find Kieran. I had to save him. It was not our time.

I closed my eyes and reached for my internal strength, pushing the dirt and roots up and away from us. I focused on creating a slope up to the forest above us and imagined it opening up to the forest floor, letting us free.

Levi gasped again. A deep breath taking air into his lungs. Roots loosened around me, retracting. Reopening my eyes, I blinked rapidly to adjust my eyes to the darkness. I watched as the earth shifted and warped away from us. A tunnel formed, sloping steeply upward.

"Come on." I said.

Levi stumbled forward, still holding me around my waist, stopping me from falling. I focused on pushing the earth back, while Levi focused on moving us both forward.

A small trail of light hit our faces. We watched the hole open wide enough for us to stagger through. The fresh air in our lungs had us both sighing in relief. Small wood animals scattered away from us and we moved to the nearest tree.

He glanced at me, putting his other arm around me to hold me upright, and gasped. "Your nose!"

"I'm okay." I waved him off. "Just too much magic."

"You saved us," Levi said, his breathing heavy, supporting me as I squatted and sat in front of the tree.

I shook my head, leaning my back and head against the tree. "I almost killed us both."

"Yes, but you got us out of that cell and out of the cave." He kneeled beside me.

"Just…" I looked at him.

"Trixie!" Jake gasped as he, Tori, and Clara stepped out from the trees.

"Oh, thank god." I muttered.

Jake raised an eyebrow. "Nope, just us."

I scoffed. "Funny."

"Are you okay? We've been so worried." Tori said, and her voice changed with shock. "What happened to your nose?"

"I'm fine. I'll explain later." I said, turning my eyes to Jake.

Jake eyed Levi; clearly he didn't understand or trust why Levi was here too.

"Long story, but Levi was locked in the cell with me and he's on our side." I said.

Jake's eyes raked over me. "Okay."

"I saw Sienna." I said carefully, watching their expressions.

"What?" Clara asked, her eyebrows furrowed.

Tori's face was expressionless as she glanced between us.

"She's alive. She's my sister."

"What?" Jake and Clara said in unison.

My eyes turned dark. "And my dad…everything was a lie."

Levi placed a hand over mine. "We're all here for you."

I turned my head and the corner of my mouth lifted slightly. Levi sat closer to me than I realised. I filled my lungs with air, glancing at Tori and Clara, and then at Jake. Jake's eyes darted to our hands and his jaw clenched. Sucking on my lips, I shifted, pulling my hand away from Levi's.

"Did you see Kieran?" Clara asked.

I shook my head. "No, we don't know if he's there or not."

I wiped at my nose. The bleeding had stopped.

"Let's get back to Myrdreya and clean you up," Jake said.

"No, we have to find Kieran." I pushed myself up to stand.

"You're no use to us if you're bleeding and weak." Clara said.

"Levi said we were in the same cave that I had been in before…" I looked at Jake and Clara, "when I had been controlled."

"How did you escape?" Tori asked, drawing all our attention to her.

I glanced at Clara momentarily before answering. "Elemental magic."

Clara snapped her eyes to mine. "You can…?"

"Yes, she's like me." Tori answered Clara's unasked question.

"Since when?" Clara injected.

"My whole life." I said, shaking my head and turning to Jake. "We're wasting time. We need to investigate where the cave is."

"You need rest." Tori said.

"Cave first, then rest." I demanded.

Tori looked at Jake. He nodded.

"Which way?" Jake asked.

Levi stood up and pointed toward the trees in the direction we had emerged from the ground.

"Be on your guard in case there are any scouts." Jake instructed before turning toward the location Levi pointed. "Let's go."

Levi stayed close to my side. I stumbled over a tree root, and he gripped me around my waist to steady me.

"Maybe you should wait here?" Levi said.

"No." I snapped. "I need to see where we had been held captive."

Jake eyed Levi's arm around me, and his jaw worked again. I've obviously got some explaining to do—but it had to wait. I swallowed and placed my arm around Levi's shoulders. We were both covered head to toe in dirt from being buried in the tunnel.

"How far did you travel from the cave?" Clara said.

Levi and I glanced at one another.

"Ten minutes or more?" Levi said, still watching me.

I nodded. "Yes, about ten minutes."

We trudged through the thickening forest. I was thankful for Levi's support in walking, but I couldn't help but feel guilty. Jake kept stealing glances back at us, making me anxious. It's not like we're doing anything wrong. We're friends now, nothing more.

Clouds covered the sky, the sun hidden from sight. The forest grew darker as we weaved through it. Birds chirped nearby and flew away as we approached.

A rock face came into view between the trees. Jake slowed and held his hand out.

"Is this it?" Jake whispered.

Tori leaned behind a tree and peered around it. Clara indicted for us to hide as well. Jake crept forward, hopping from tree to tree to get closer. Levi hauled us behind a wide oak trunk. I took my arm off Levi and gripped the tree. He released my waist, but he stayed close. I peered around the trunk, watching Jake.

He stopped behind a tree and put his finger to his lips to tell us all to keep quiet. His gaze went blank—and I knew exactly what he was doing.

My head was heavy, but I refused to give in. I focused ahead and pushed out my senses, too.

Trees, birds and rocks. Ivy leaves hung over the rock face. *Where was the cave?* A small waterfall to the left, some fish in the water and insects around the surface. I pushed my sense to the right. *There.* It was barely visible—thick ivy leaves covered the entrance.

Kieran could be in there. My fingers gripped into the bark as I pushed my senses forward, through the leaves and into the cave. At first I saw nothing, but then dull light lit up the walls of the cave further down.

My heart thrummed faster, and I pushed further into the cave, the lights getting brighter. *Kieran, where are you?* I vaguely heard my name but ignored it.

The lights went out, throwing me into darkness. Arms wrapped around me tightly. The bark no longer touching my fingers. Everything faded and I couldn't hear or see anything but black.

Sixteen

TRIXIE

THE WARMTH OF SUNLIGHT TOUCHED my skin. Softness under my body told me I was back in my bed. *Ah, the comfort of Kieran's bed.* His bed was always so comfortable. I reached beside me, but the sheets were cold and empty.

My eyes snapped open, and I bolted upright.

"Kieran?" I called out.

The room was empty. *Of course it was.* He wasn't here. Memories of the previous adventures flowed through my mind. *Shit. How long had I been sleeping?*

I hurried out of bed. Looking down at myself, the dirt and any reminiscence of the capture and tunnel escape were gone. I was clean and dressed in a shirt and shorts. *Who had cleaned and dressed me?* My stomach dropped at the thought.

I shook my head and headed for the wardrobe. Picking out a pair of long black pants and a lilac singlet, I shrugged out of the bed wear and undergarments and re-dressed. I brushed my hair and donned a pair of black sneakers before opening the bedroom door and stopping short.

Clara sat on the floor, her back leaning against the wall. She looked up at me and pushed herself to stand.

"Good sleep?" she asked, walking over to me.

I nodded and eyed her curiously. "How long have I been asleep?"

"Um, about eight hours."

"WHAT?" I yelled louder than I had intended.

She put her hands up. "You needed it. You drained yourself to the point of almost stopping your heart. You have no idea how much you scared us all."

My jaw slackened, and I stared at her wary expression.

"I gave you a wipe down to remove the visible dirt, and dressed you." She said.

I swallowed and bit my lip.

"Don't worry, I didn't take off your undies and bra, so I saw nothing. I just didn't want to spread dirt on your bed." She explained.

Well, that's that question answered.

"Thank you." I said, nodding.

Her mouth quirked up at the side in a half smile. "You're welcome."

"So, what have I missed?" I asked, closing the door behind me.

"After the healer tended to you and—."

"Wait, a healer?" I abruptly interrupted her.

She nodded and started down the corridor. I followed her lead and walked beside her.

"Yes, we have a Soul Weaver with a gift of healing. It has its limits, though, like anything." She gave me a stern glare before continuing. "She can only heal minor wounds, but she's also got some healing tonics to help. Once we were satisfied that you were recovering, Jake, Tori and I returned to the cave."

"Did you find him?" I gripped Clara's forearm.

Clara stopped walking and looked down at my hand.

"Sorry." I let go of her arm hastily.

She sighed. "They were gone. It was empty."

"No, no, no…"

"I'm sorry Trixie. Kieran wasn't there." She began walking again, heading around the corner. "But we don't think he had ever been there."

My breath caught in my throat, and I almost forgot to breathe. I inhaled and hurried to catch up to Clara.

"What do we do now?" I asked frantically.

She was silent for a long moment as we rounded another corner and exited the mansion. "There's something else you should know."

My heart pounded in my ears as I waited for her to continue.

"Your father…Levi was right." She said, watching my face. "He left the city. Mae said he left soon after we did."

The dryness in my mouth made my throat raw as the air passing through. I stared ahead of us. Despite the betrayal from my father all over again, no tears came. Instead of the hurt I should have felt, I balled up my fists and ground my teeth. Fury built up inside my very being.

There was no room to cry. No room for forgiveness. No love left for them anymore. They were not my parents. They only ever cared for my sister, not for me.

They will pay for destroying my life; from my childhood to adulthood. They ruined me. And it was my turn to ruin them.

"Are you okay?" Clara watched me from the corner of her eye.

Before I could answer or even think of what to answer, Tori and Jake came into view. I relaxed my fists as they approached us.

"How are you feeling?" Tori asked. I didn't miss the quick glance she threw at Clara.

I answered her with another question. "So, he wasn't in the cave?"

Clara swallowed, saying nothing. I glanced between each of their faces; Clara, Jake, and Tori.

"Where's Levi?" I asked, my brows knitting together.

"He's fine." Clara answered quickly.

"He's currently in the training grounds." Jake said, his gaze brushed over me.

Well, at least someone was fine. I sure as hell wasn't. And Kieran, *was he still alive?* My heart sank to the pit of my stomach and I thought I would vomit. Spinning away from them, I bent over, dry reaching.

"Trixie, are you sure you're okay?" Tori asked. "Maybe you should go lay back down."

The glass below my feet looked thicker and more textured than usual. I blinked. Head spinning, stomach heaving, the lightest touch of a hand on my shoulder. I forced myself upright and turned—but it wasn't Tori, Clara or Jake I saw. It was Kieran.

Blood drained from my face, my skin turning cold and clammy. Everything holding me together crumpled into nothingness.

Shackles still held his wrists above his head, while his legs dangled limply. His body covered from fingers to toes with gashes thick with dirt and blood. His chin on his chest, red dripping from his mouth. The larger wound on his back wept. *Oh no.* His wounds were becoming infected. We were running out of time.

A movement from the left broke my attention on Kieran. I stared at the woman who shared my eyes and cheekbones—Sienna. Hatred rippled through my muscles. She paced and stopped, her eyes sweeping over the room.

"I will find you." I said through my gritted teeth.

Sienna's mouth curled at the corner. She gripped Kieran's hair in her fist and pulled his head up. He had a short, deep cut on his cheek, running close to his left eye. I gasped.

"Trixie? Trixie?" I vaguely heard my name being called, but it wasn't Sienna or Kieran.

"Get away from him." I screamed, stepping forward and reaching for Kieran.

Sienna's eyes snapped to mine. I froze. My eyes widened and my heart threatened to burst from my rib cage.

"What are you going to do about it?" she smirked.

"Can you hear me, Trixie?" The voice called for me.

I shook my head, ignoring the shouts for my attention and composing my shock.

"When I find you, I'm going to kill you." I growled.

Her mouth only widened. "I doubt that. You're weak and vulnerable."

"I wouldn't underestimate me." I warned.

"Trixie!" Shouting reached my ears. "You have to stop!"

"You can't touch me." Sienna taunted.

I leapt forward and placed my hands on her shoulders. I was instantly blasted off my feet and I was falling. Blinking rapidly, flashes of scenery blocked my vision. None of it I recognised.

My body shook—no, just my shoulders. The dark green landscape transformed into glass. Glass spikes surrounded me—us.

I stared at Tori, who shook me by the shoulders.

"Tori?" I whispered.

Tori's eyes softened as she stared back at me, but mine widened when I looked around us. Glass surrounded us. Clara and Jake were nowhere in sight, but I could hear their voices shouting.

"She's alright!" Tori yelled without taking her eyes off me.

The glass was close to us, but not touching. I swept my eyes over her and relief washed over me when I saw no injuries.

"Focus." Tori said calmly, still gripping my shoulders.

I sucked in a breath and pushed against the glass. It warped back into the ground.

Jake and Clara bolted to us.

"We're out of time." I shuddered, a tear running down my cheek.

"He's not dead." Jake stated, his hands balled into fists at his sides.

"No." I whispered.

"What did you see?" Tori demanded.

"Sienna, she could see me."

Tori's eyes widened. "What?"

"Kieran," I shook my head, "covered in blood."

"What else?" Tori pushed.

My eyebrows knitted together. "I saw dark mountains. They were almost black. And a castle…by the sea."

Tori dropped her hands from my shoulders and stepped back.

"There's only one castle in Zalindor…" Jake said. "And it's been deserted for hundreds of years."

"Not anymore." Tori's voice barely reached our ears.

We all stared at Tori, waiting for an explanation.

"I should have thought of it before." Tori closed her eyes and pinched the bridge of her nose.

"Of what?" Jake pressed, stepping closer to her.

Tori sighed, her eyes flickering to Jake, then back to me. "When I left Myrdreya, I headed south. I thought I would explore areas I hadn't been before…the deserted black castle."

My eyebrows knitted together as the map Kieran had showed me came into my mind. The castle was down south, between the mountains and the ocean. Jake and Clara glanced at one another.

"It's not crumbling anymore. Someone has mended it." Tori continued. Her gaze drifted back to Jake. "The watch tower closest to it, it was manned…they must have been Dark Soul Weavers."

"Do you think…?" I started, swallowing the lump in my throat. I couldn't finish my question.

"Yes." Tori answered, her gaze flicking to me again. "Julianne has to be there. And…I think Kieran must be too."

"Well, what are we waiting for? Let's go!" I turned toward the mansion, but a hand gripped around my wrist and pulled me back.

Tori held onto me, holding my gaze. "You can't go there without having full control of your emotions and your gifts."

"What?" I breathed. "I cannot sit here and do nothing while he could be dying."

"You won't be doing nothing…technically." Levi said.

I shot him a glare, and he raised his eyebrows. *When had he even joined us?*

"We will all need to prepare before walking into that castle. It's a maze in there and we have to expect the worst." Clara said.

"Trixie…" Tori began, but I would be damned if I was staying behind.

"I'm not staying behind." I said through gritted teeth, prying my wrist from her grip. "You cannot make me. If you leave here, I will find my own way there."

"She can do it." Levi said, drawing everyone's eyes on him. "She had a vision in the cell we were held in, and then she warped us through the wall and through a tunnel away from the cave."

None of us spoke. All eyes were on Levi, waiting for him to continue.

"We were almost buried alive in that tunnel. She…" his voice trailed off, and he looked over my face.

"I had used so much magic to get us out that I lost it." I dropped my eyes away from Levi, staring off into the distance. "The dirt warped back around us, and…even though I panicked, I couldn't let us die there. I couldn't die there without saving Kieran first. I found my willpower to push the dirt back and release us, then I dug the tunnel to the surface, where we escaped into the forest."

Levi nodded. "We had only escaped minutes before you guys found us."

Tori bit her lip, her eyes full of wander. Clara and Jake both wore a half smile. My eyes set on Tori and turned to fully face her.

"Between your training and my willpower to save Kieran, I can do this." I said, watching her expression closely.

She sighed and nodded. "You have to show us that what just happened won't happen again."

I took a deep breath and nodded.

"Okay," Clara said. "Tori, you work with Trixie. Jake and I will go do some research on the ancient magic that Sienna clearly possesses."

Clara and Jake turned to leave, but Levi's voice cut in.

"What should I do?" He said, his hands hanging by his sides, palms facing forward.

Clara and Jake exchanged a quick glance.

"You can be Trixie's motivation." Clara said, raising her eyebrows at Tori before turning away.

I watched Clara and Jake disappear into the mansion. I returned my gaze to Levi, and we shared the same confusion.

"Come on." Tori said, heading toward the gardens.

I shrugged, and we followed Tori.

⋙◉⋘

"OKAY, YOU'LL HAVE to explain how I'm her motivation." Levi said, as we entered the gardens.

"Well," Tori started as she turned to face us. "Believe it or not, she does still care about you."

I avoided Levi's gaze, keeping my eyes focused on Tori. I could feel Levi's eyes on my face. She wasn't wrong. I will always care for him, just not in the way I used to.

"Soooo…I'm going to attack you and she's going to defend you using her warping ability." Tori said in a matter-of-a-fact tone.

My eyes widened slightly, and I gritted my teeth. Levi raised his eyebrows and looked at me pointedly.

The glass beneath our feet shifted. It cracked, and bolts of glass shot up around us in an endless wave of spikes. If it had been an actual attack, it would be horrifying.

Tori's face was calm, but her eyes told another

story—she was determined. I looked at Levi and the spikes were growing closer and closer to him.

"You won't hurt him," I said.

Tori arched an eyebrow. "Won't I?"

She pushed the spikes closer. They were surrounding him—no escape. Levi stood still, his eyes flickering from spike to spike as they threatened him.

One particular spike grew longer and weaved its way around Levi's wrist before he could react. He stared at it, as did I. The glass spike spawned thorns from the ground—one by one they appeared and grew along the spike toward Levi's wrist.

My eyes grew wide. "Tori..."

"You might want to hurry." Tori taunted.

I ground my teeth and watched as a thorn spiked at his skin, pricking a drop of blood from his wrist.

"Tori, don't—."

"You better stop talking and get warping." Tori said, cutting me off.

Shit. She really was going to hurt him. Another thorn hit his wrist and more blood spilled.

Levi groaned. "Trix, I don't think she's bluffing."

"I know." I growled back at him.

I focused on the spike and thorns wrapping around his bloodied wrist. I almost suffocated him—us—in that tunnel. Despite needing to practice my gift, I wasn't about to let Tori harm him.

More blood spilled as a third thorn dug into his skin

and he let out a hiss. *Fuck. Okay, I can do this.* I cleared my mind and focused on removing the thorns from his skin. One by one, the thorns shrank back into the spike.

A moment of pride filled my chest. But, it was short-lived. The thorns grew back and stabbed in his wrist deeper.

"Anytime now, Trix." Levi said through clenched teeth.

Because it was that easy. He did not know how much concentration and power it took. *Or did it not? Was I overthinking it?* I bit my lip and pushed against the glass, concentrating on the transparent material dissolving away and back into the ground.

I could feel the pressure of the glass and how it was being told to do one thing by Tori and another thing by me. I pushed harder, and the glass shattered.

I blinked as the glass fell to the ground and warped back into place. My eyes hovered over Levi, stopping at his wrist, a small amount of blood dripping from it.

"Next time, believe me, I will hurt him." Tori said, stepping toward Levi.

I saw her movement and instantly snapped my eyes to her. Glass vines grew up from the ground, separating her from Levi. Tori stopped and eyed me.

"I was only going to check his wounds." She said.

I breathed hard, holding the barrier in place, and said, "Try to break through."

Tori inclined her head to me. "Very well."

She pushed against it. Every vine she broke, I replaced it with a new one. When she stepped sideways, I grew more vines blocking her movement. Her expression grew frustrated.

Minutes passed, and she had failed to break through. Levi stood quiet the entire time, watching as Tori and I silently had a warping war.

Tori dropped her chin, and her face calmed. The corner of her mouth lifted, and she gazed over to me.

"Nice work, Trixie." She said. "Your willpower to keep up the defence is more powerful than me breaking through."

I grinned and released the glass. The ground was once more whole again.

"Now, I want you to really gain control of warping the glass to save Levi." Tori said, pacing in front of us.

I groaned. *Not again.*

"Levi will be trying to hide. I will be perusing him. You need to warp the surroundings to stop me from getting to him without actually harming me."

I flinched at the last part. *What if I did hurt her?* And badly. Jake would never forgive me. I swallowed, the beating of my heart thumping against my ribs.

"Off you go Levi, stay within the gardens." Tori flicked a hand at Levi.

Levi nodded and left us alone together. Tori turned to me.

"Right, warp walls, vines, that kind of thing to stop

me from getting near him. Don't overthink it." Her eyes bore into mine for a long moment before she turned and ran after Levi.

Oh shit. I bolted after her. She neared a glass bush to the right, so I focused on it. The branches grew and blocked her pathway. She dived to the left around them. Levi crouched behind a statue and Tori was heading right for it.

My eyes shot to the ground beneath her feet. It began to ripple and sway, causing her to topple sideways. She almost lost her footing, but jumped and regained her balance. *Dammit.* I pushed spikes up from the ground a metre in front of Tori. She skidded to a halt and stepped back. Her head flicked side to side as she searched for another way around.

Levi peered around the statue. His body was visible but distorted behind the glass. In that moment of distraction, Tori warped her way through my spike wall. *Shit, she's good.* I ran forward after her.

Tori was gaining ground toward Levi. *No.* I couldn't let her win. If she won, then she wouldn't agree that I was ready to go to the black castle. Putting all my concentration on the ground in front and behind Tori, I grew vines that wrapped around her legs and arms, halting her movement completely.

Yes! I formed more vines, creating a thick cage around her. Focusing hard on the glass, I held it in place even as she pushed against it with her own elemental magic. I walked up to her, sidestepping around her, and smirked as her eyes locked onto mine.

"So, am I ready yet?" I raised my eyebrows and crossed my arms.

"You tell me." She replied, and her mouth grew into a grin that reached right to her ears.

Seventeen

KIERAN

EVERYTHING HURT. Bruised and bleeding from hands to feet. I moved in out of consciousness, barely aware of my surroundings half the time. *Had it been days, weeks, months?* I didn't know.

"How much more are you going to suffer before she comes?" Sienna tilted her head. "Maybe she won't come at all. Maybe your life means nothing to her."

I spat blood on the stone floor in front of me. It only added to the building a pool of red. A part of me hoped Trixie would stay away. Would let me die. I didn't want her to see me like this. I didn't want her to suffer the same fate.

I still didn't understand what they wanted with her. *Why cause her all this suffering to kill her?*

What if she never came? My stomach churned as the heat in my veins spread, burning me from the inside out. *Would they finally kill me to end my suffering? Would it be quick, or would they make me suffer for as long as Trixie had?*

"I think we need to get her attention," Sienna's eyes darkened and her mouth turned up in a cruel smirk, "don't you?"

I attempted to swallow the growing lump in my throat, but it wouldn't budge.

Sienna stepped closer. Her hand turned molten. Smoke rising and fire licking her fingertips. *Here we go again.* I sucked in a lung full of air and waited for the agony.

She touched my chest with her forefinger, and my skin seared. I gritted my teeth, keeping my eyes locked on hers.

Sienna was pure evil. There was nothing about her remotely similar to Trixie. The kind hearted soul of Trixie was completely absent in her sister. For so many years, we thought Julianne and Jay were the cruelty in our world when the real perpetrator was Sienna.

She pressed her palm to my bare chest, and I roared in excruciating pain. If I didn't have the thought of Trixie grounding me, I would have given up long ago. If I gave up, they would find her. She meant everything to me, and I wasn't letting her family destroy her.

My breathing faltered as the fire burned into my chest. The flames scorched my skin, and the burning spread through my veins. I clenched my jaw and groaned.

"How does it feel to be burning from the inside out?" Sienna taunted.

She lifted her hand off my chest, but the burning continued. It always continued for hours afterwards. She stepped closer, her evil smirk widening.

"What would Trixie think of you if your face was spoiled?" her eyes wandered over my eyes, nose, and lips. "You wouldn't be the handsome man you are. Would she still love you? Would she leave you and go back to Levi?"

I swallowed, my breathing quickening. It was no use avoiding Sienna. There was nowhere to go. I stared at her as her hand came toward my face. She pushed her entire hand against my right cheek. The searing started with the contact and I roared.

Eighteen

I RESTED FOR THE REMAINING of the afternoon. Tori's instructions. After dinner, we congregated around a table in Jake's room, boring over the map of Zalindor.

"What if we enter from here?" Clara pointed to a section on the map.

Tori shook her head. "No, this tower will see us."

Frustration seeped through my bones. We had been staring at the parchment for hours and were no closer to a plan to rescue Kieran than we were when we started.

I pushed away from the table and paced the room. There must be a way, we just needed to find it.

"What if we looked at it from this angle?" Jake said, pointing at something on the map I was too far away to see. "We could keep to the mountains by the water here…"

I stopped pacing, snapping my eyes to Jake's back.

"No, they station guards up in this corner of the castle to patrol that area." Tori shot down another suggestion.

A new angle. That was what we needed. Mountains. Water. I hurried back over to the map, staring down at it.

"We're looking at it from the wrong angle." I said.

Their heads turned toward me, but they stayed silent.

"We can't teleport directly into the castle because they've warded the walls and plus we wouldn't want to give them access to jump through our port into Myrdreya." I recited our previous findings. "We can't enter the area on the land either, because no matter where we come from, they will see us and their wards will stop us from getting in."

Jake and Clara stared at me with disgruntled expressions.

"But we haven't thought about entering from—."

"The water." Tori finished, smiling at me.

I nodded. "Yes. We can swim and—."

"The towers will see us swimming." Clara interrupted.

"Not if we're diving underwater and then warping

through the sand and up into the castle floor." I explained.

Clara and Jake exchanged a look.

"That...might actually work." Jake said, looking at Tori.

Tori nodded. "I think that will be our best shot. We need to get some diving gear from the mainland."

"I can organise that." Levi said.

I looked over my shoulder at him. I had forgotten he was in the room. He hadn't spoken in an hour.

"I'll go with you." Clara said. "I can port us there and back."

Levi nodded. "I know exactly where we can get them."

"Okay, let's go." Clara crossed the room, passing Levi.

Levi gave me a small smile and turned to follow Clara out the door. I watched the door close before turning back to Jake and Tori.

"You need to practise warping underground without burning out." Tori said, crossing her arms.

I shook my head. "We don't have time for that. I need to go rest to gain my strength before we leave tomorrow."

Jake raised his eyebrows. "I guess you're right. You need rest, and we need to go as soon as we can."

Tori sighed. "Let's go get some sleep, Trixie. We both will need as much strength as we can."

"TRIXIE," A soft voice said beside me. "It's time."

I snapped my eyes open. Tori was standing over my bed, fully dressed in fighting gear. I blinked my sleep away and sat up in the darkness.

"What time is it?" I rubbed my eyes.

"Around 5am." Tori stepped back and pointed to the clothes on the end of my bed. "Get dressed. We'll meet you at the portal room. Pack as many daggers as you can carry."

"I only have one." I said, and when Tori frowned, I explained. "Kieran hasn't taught me how to fight with daggers yet."

Tori nodded. "Alright, well, bring that and I'll give you a couple more at the portal. We might need them."

I climbed out of bed, and Tori left the room. Quickly pulling on the fighting the gear she had laid out for me, I smiled. My moment of satisfaction disappeared as quickly as it came. *Was Kieran okay?* My lips pressed into a hard line. If he was...I couldn't even think about it. I wouldn't want to continue. I wouldn't want to make it out of there alive if he wasn't.

Shaking my head, I moved to buckle my boots. I slipped my dagger inside my jacket and zipped it up. My fingers trekked through my hair and I pulled it all to one side. Entwining my fingers through it, I plaited it to keep it tamed for the swim.

A few minutes later, I was out of the room and heading for the portal room. When I arrived, Tori and Jake were standing closely together talking. I smiled to myself. I peered around the room and saw Levi leaning against the wall a few metres away. He nodded to me. The shadows under eyes suggested he hadn't slept. Next to him was a pile of bags.

I raised my eyebrows. "Diving gear?"

"Yep. I paid them off to cover the cost of buying new gear." Levi said.

I nodded. "Makes sense, as I doubt we'll bring it back with us."

Levi chuckled. "My thoughts exactly."

I gave him a half smile before turning to Tori and Jake. Clara wasn't here yet. Jake and Tori broke conversation and walked over to me.

"Clara will be here soon." Jake said. "We'll port to the north side of the Igor Mountains, by the ocean, and go into the water from there."

"How will we know how far to swim?" I asked.

Levi put his hand into his pocket and pulled out a compact device, holding it up. "With this. It's an underwater gps."

I nodded. Tori held something out to me. Two daggers in sheaths rested on her palm.

"Some extra daggers, as promised." Tori said.

I took one from her, unsheathing it. The hilt was plain

dark green with one green gem. The blade interested me most; it was jagged, like a zigzag with intricate ivy leaf patterns. I glowered as I held the hilt in my hand, a perfect fit for my small hands.

"Ivy is my oldest dagger." Tori smiled.

My jaw dropped open slightly. "Ivy?"

Tori nodded. "That's her name."

"You name your daggers?"

"Yes, I do. She's the first dagger I ever owned and I would like you to have it."

I shook my head, sheathing the beauty and holding it back to her. "No, I couldn't."

Tori held up her free hand. "Please, it's yours. I've got a new favourite…a dagger Jake gave me."

Jake shifted beside her, his eyes on Tori. "You still have Ember?"

Tori held out the other dagger in her palm for me to take. I took the second dagger and Tori's hand moved to her jacket to pull out another dagger. The sheath was black with a red and orange flame. She slid the dagger out for us all to see.

The hilt was a gradient of black to red, to orange. The silver blade protruding from it started with licks of flame shaped metal, morphing into a curved point.

A whoosh of air left my lungs. "That's…"

"Extravagant." Jake whispered. "Just like its owner."

Tori's eyes found his. The malice I saw in her eyes whenever she looked at him when I met her was long gone. Jake's lips turned up in a sad smile, but his eyes had nothing but affection for her. Tori's eyes twinkled with something I hadn't seen in them before, but she was expressionless.

Unzipping my jacket, I placed Ivy in a spare inner pocket. I unsheathed the second dagger. This one had a black straight blade with silver swirls and a plain black hilt. It was simple, yet elegant.

"Storm." Tori's eyes locked onto the blade in my hands. "My mother's blade. This one I trust you'll return."

I nodded. "Definitely. I'll look after Ivy and Storm."

Tori smiled.

"Here," Levi opened one of the bags and pulled out several pairs of…soft socks?

I frowned, staring at him.

"Soft cotton shoes," Levi said to my confused expression, "they can be worn with the flippers, so we at least have something protecting our feet in the castle."

"We ready to go?" Clara entered the portal room as I homed the dagger inside my jacket.

"As ready as we can be," Jake replied.

We all moved to collect our cotton shoes and swap them for our boots. They were thin, but they were better than nothing.

A moment later, Mae walked into the room.

"I see you're all here, ready?" Mae said, gazing at us all.

We nodded in unison. Levi and Jake picked up the bags and Tori pocketed Ember.

"Remember, when we arrive, we put on the diving gear and get into the water quickly." Jake said. "We don't want to be out in the open longer than necessary."

We nodded in agreement, and Mae created the portal in front of us. A dark cliff face and forest swirled in the portal. This was it. It was time to finally rescue Kieran.

Nineteen

THE DARK MOUNTAIN SIDE AND forest surrounding us were more ominous in person—especially at this time of morning. Briars entwined along the base of the mountains, extending halfway up the sides, blocking any attempt to climb the range.

"This way." Jake pointed to the southeast.

We followed Jake in silence, treading through the marsh and to the edge of the thinning trees within minutes. On high alert, our eyes scouted the area. Clara's and Jake's eyes glazed over as they scouted with their senses.

"Clear." Clara said.

Jake nodded and turned to Levi. "Alright, let's get into our suits."

Levi and Jake dropped the large bags at their feet, unzipping them and pouring out the contents.

"I had to guess the sizes best I could," Levi said, grouping all the flippers into a pile to his right. "Sorry if I guessed wrong, it will have to do."

Clara bent down and helped Levi group the suits for each person. They handed them out and everyone began dressing.

"Zipper goes at the back." Levi said as he pulled his own suit up his legs over his clothes. "Pull it all the way up to your waist, put both arms in and then pull it up to your neck. Use the string to zip it up, then put the canister on your back, fastening the buckles."

Following his instructions, we were all dressed in our wetsuits ready to go. Levi threw the bag aside and turned the GPS on. I assumed he was keying in the coordinates of our destination.

"Alright, put your flippers and masks on once you're in the water." Levi instructed, picking up his own set. "Put the mouthpiece in before you dive and turn on your canister."

We waded into the shallows with our flippers, and masks tucked under our elbows. Clara and Jake had a dagger each in their free hand—just in case, I guessed. After fitting our flippers and masks, we lowered into the water. One by one, we put the mouthpiece in, turned on our oxygen, and dived under.

Levi led us. We dove and swam in single file, heading south along the mountainside. Besides the occasional fish, we didn't see any other life amongst the sea water.

After what felt like half an hour, Levi pointed to the right. The sandy bed turned to pebbles and rock. We swam toward the rocks Levi pointed. Tori and I glanced at one another before moving forward and stopping right in front of the rocks.

Tori nodded and together we pushed against the rocks with our minds, warping the rocks into a tunnel until we reached dirt. We opened it enough for us all to fit into the tunnel. Tori waved a hand at the others behind us as I pushed forward.

Opening the tunnel further and holding it in place, I turned to watch as Tori worked to close us off from the ocean. Once the rocks were back in place, the sand followed, blocking the stone from sight. I put my attention back on the tunnel ahead of us.

Pushing against the dirt, I cleared the tunnel deeper into the earth. The ocean water began to drain, soaking into the dirt. As the water dispersed, we planted our flippers down on the ground and our heads rose above the water. I pulled the piece out of the mouth and removed the mask, dropping them into the water. I watched as the others did the same.

Tori focused on holding the walls of the tunnel away from us, and I slipped the scuba diving pack from my back. It fell in the water and I started shrugging out of the wetsuit. They weren't made for wearing such gear underneath them. It clung to the clothes I wore beneath it.

The water had drained into the soil down to our waists. Jake and Levi had successfully removed their suits and abandoned them in the water. Clara had hers down to her ankles and was pulling it off one foot. I bent over to push mine down over my knees, but I toppled, sending a splash of water toward Jake and Levi as I fell beneath the surface.

Hands gripped around my arms and torso, pulling me back above the water. I gulped a lungful of air and stared up at Levi and Jake.

"Are you okay?" Levi asked, his hand around my waist.

I nodded. "Thank you. I slipped."

"Hold her." Jake said, bending down. "I'll pull the wetsuit off."

"Thanks." I placed an arm around Levi's shoulders and lifted a foot for Jake.

A few swift movements and Jake had the suit off me. Levi made sure I was steady on my feet before releasing me. I looked over to Clara; she was watching us with a curious expression on her face.

"Alright," I said. "Tori, your turn."

I stepped up beside her and focused on the dirt in the tunnel, pushing it away from us. By the time Tori had removed her wetsuit, the water had drained down to our ankles.

"Time to move forward." Tori said.

Together, Tori and I used our gifts to wrap the earth, and we followed Levi's gps to the castle. Walking in eerie silence, the only sound penetrating our ears were our soaked cloth shoes on dirt and the rustle of our wet clothes.

My chest tightened. We panted as we continued forward. Heart pounding harder, threatening to burst from my ribs, I weakened. Warping took an amazingly huge amount of power. I looked at Tori. With so many more years of experience than me, she warped through with much more ease. Although, a bead of sweat rolled down her forehead.

I glanced over my shoulder at the others. Levi looked like he would pass out soon. Clara fanned her face with her hand, and Jake had removed his jacket, carrying it over his shoulder. He looked as sweaty and sticky as I felt.

"We're almost there." Levi muttered, staring down at the gps in his hands.

A whoosh of air escaped my lungs. I had been longing to hear those words. *Had it been an hour?* No, I didn't think so. Maybe about half an hour. Either way, it was taking too long, and we were tiring.

"Just a bit further." Tori muttered; she sounded as relieved as I felt.

I pushed hard against the soil. Tree roots made an appearance here and there in the upper parts of the dirt tunnel.

"We need to go a little lower, then when we get under the castle, we go up." Tori said.

I nodded and focused on the dirt toward the ground, pushing it downward. Our tunnel sloped down.

"That will do." Tori said after a few metres and we levelled the tunnel off again.

"Another five metres and we'll be under the castle, in the north-eastern corner." Levi announced.

We all heaved a relieved sigh. But the task ahead was nothing to be relieved about. We didn't know exactly what we would be facing. And we didn't know where in the dungeon we will break into. All we knew was that the dungeon was in the north-eastern corner of the castle and Kieran was most likely to be there.

We shifted the dirt five more metres and then pushed the tunnel upwards.

"Right here. We need to go up." Levi stated.

Tori and I glanced at one another.

"Alright, let's do this," Tori said. "I'll break through above us. You create steps below so we can climb.

Tori turned her focused on the earth above us, and I looked around at our feet. *Alright, I can do this.* I etched a step into the side of our tunnel. Smiling at my handwork, I dug out another step just above it, creating a dirt ladder.

I glanced up and saw grey stone emerging from the dirt. The stone shifted aside, wedging into the earth as a hole opened up. Looking over my shoulder, I saw Levi stuff the gps into a pocket and pull out his dagger. Jake adorned his jacket and pulled his sword out of its sheath. Clara was already holding a dagger in one hand and staring up into the hole.

I tore my eyes from them and finished with the stairs, focusing on holding them in place while Tori focused on holding the tunnel and the hole in place.

Clara nodded to Jake. "Go. There's no one nearby."

She must have already used her senses to check our surroundings. Jake climbed the makeshift ladder and peered out through the opening. He only paused for a moment before he placed his sword on the stone ground and pulled himself up. Clara followed him directly after.

"Your turn." I looked at Levi.

Levi nodded and climbed the ladder. The tunnel shrunk behind us; the earth resettling back into place. The space we stood in now was tiny.

"Alright, Trixie." Tori said. "I'll hold this, you climb and then I come straight after you."

I swallowed. "Okay."

I reached up and gripped the stone above with my hands and placed a foot on the first step. Climbing the steps, I held onto the stone and heaving myself up. I sat on my knees at the edge of the opening, peering back down. Tori was already climbing.

Tori gasped and looked down. I followed her gaze. The dirt below her had begun to fill in. It had caught around one of her feet.

Jake reached down to grab Tori's wrists. Her hands clasped around his wrists, and he heaved her upwards. Her foot released. Jake wrapped his arms around her waist and lifted her out of the earth. As soon as she was clear from the opening, the stone caved in and became a solid floor again.

I let out a rush of air and looked up at Tori. She was in Jake's arms and they were looking at each other. Unspoken words exchanged between them.

I smiled slightly before pushing myself to stand and taking in our surroundings. We had warped ourselves into a dungeon cell. I looked around the stone room. No bed, a cobweb in the upper back corner and a metal door with bars on it stood ajar across the room.

"I guess we're in the dungeons." I bit my lip.

Clara stepped toward the doorway and froze. Her body tensed and she spun herself against the wall soundlessly, a finger flying to her lips. Jake dragged Tori to the wall next to Clara. Levi gripped my hand and lead me against the wall opposite the doorway.

We listened as footsteps came closer to our cell, pressing ourselves as far against the stone as possible. The boots slowed as they neared. Only mildly conscious of Levi still holding my hand, I didn't dare move.

I breathed slow breaths, avoiding the attention being brought to me. Out of the corner of my eye, I saw the movement I dreaded. A man with sandy blonde hair walked through the doorway and stood a few paces inside the room. If he turned, he would see us all.

I glanced over at Clara. She was dragging a dagger out of its sheath.

"Hmph." The man shook his head. "I must be hearing things."

He began turning, and Clara lunged. Her dagger hit home in the man's side. He grunted and grabbed at his injured side. Jake swung a foot out at the man's calves. His knees buckled.

"What—." The man began.

Without thinking, I froze the man in time. No. I froze everyone in the room. *Shit.* Clara and Jake slowly turned their gazes on me, eyes widening. The man was falling to the ground. I jumped forward, grabbing him under the arms. Struggling under his weight, I laid him on the ground quietly so he didn't bring more attention to us.

I stood and stretched my back.

"Sorry..." I mumbled to my friends.

I stepped backward, away from the man on the ground. His sherry eyes stared wide with shock and panic. The Soul Weaver's branding was half visible under his collar. But he was no Soul Weaver. He was a Dark Soul Weaver.

I pulled the glorious Ivy from my jacket and bent down to him with the blade against his throat. The green gem glistened.

"Move or make a sound and I'll cut your throat." I said through gritted teeth.

His hand twitched, and I glanced up at Clara and Jake. They had stepped forward, but were moving ever so slowly. *What an idiot.* Definitely not one of my finest decisions. *What if someone had heard? What if more of them came and everyone else was still slowed?*

But no one came. My friends gained more movement in the next few minutes, and so did the man held on the ground with my dagger. I kept my eyes on him and the blade. A bead of red appeared when he swallowed.

"Here's an idea." Jake said, moving to stand opposite me. "Don't do that again."

I nodded, not sparing a glance at him. "Sorry."

"How did you do that?" Clara asked beside me.

"It's another one of her gifts." Levi stepped up on my other side.

Tori moved around the man's legs and stood next to Jake. "You know, you could have told us."

"Kieran knows." I muttered.

Jake frowned momentarily and exchanged a quick look with Clara. Their frustrated demeanour vanished as quickly as it came.

"What do we do with him?" Levi asked.

Clara looked down and crouched at his hip. When

she stood, a set of keys were dangling from her fingers.

I smiled.

"That will have to do." Jake said. "It's either that or we kill him."

The man shook his head violently, but quickly stopped when the metal pierced his skin. He groaned and frozen under my blade.

The stones wobbled around him and tendrils sprouted up and over the man's body, holding him in place. I looked up at Tori and she smirked. I released the dagger from his throat and straightened.

"The hall is empty." Clara's head was cocked to one side. "Let's go."

We stepped away from the man, exiting the cell into the long passageway. Tori concentrated on holding the man captive in his stone bindings. After fumbling to find the correct key, Clara locked the cell door and Tori relaxed. The bindings released from his body and he sat up.

"Yell, and you'll wish you hadn't." Jake warned, his dark eyes eyeing the man.

The man frowned, crossing his ankles and leaning back on the palms of his hands as he eyed us.

I examined the hallway. One way lead toward a set of stairs, with a few cell doors along the way. The other way was lined with doors with one door at the far end, which only had a small window to look through. My heart hammered in my chest. *Would Kieran be in there? Were we too late?* I subconsciously started walking down the hallway.

"Trix—?" Levi began.

I turned. Clara's hand was clamped over Levi's mouth. With a stern expression, she put a finger to her lips. Levi nodded, and she dropped her hand. I returned to my path toward the metal door at the end of the hall. I sensed someone close behind me, although I didn't bother to check who.

Tori leaned over to me and whispered in my ear. "Do you think he's in that one?"

"I recognise it from my visions." I whispered back.

We slowly crept toward the door. Thanks to our cloth shows, our footsteps were almost soundless. I glanced over my shoulder. Jake and Clara were checking the other cells along the way, while maintaining watch on the stairs. Levi hung back by the cell we arrived in, his dagger in hand, watching the man while stealing glimpses at me.

I stepped lightly on the stone floor, my heart beating harder the nearer we became. The dungeon was eerily silent. The soft padding of our feet and our breathing were the only sounds reaching our ears. As we passed, the doors stood ajar and the cells I briefly looked into were empty.

Tori and I finally reached the end, the perilous metal door beckoning us to enter. Tori drew out her daggers, one in each hand. I still clutched Ivy in my right hand with a slither of drying blood on the blade. We glanced at each other for a split second before I took a breath and tried the handle. It clicked open. I frowned. *Why would it be unlocked?* Pushing the heavy door inwards, we stepped in with our daggers at the ready.

Empty.

The cell was empty. Wrist shackles were hanging from the tall ceiling. A small window on the right wall. My stomach churned as my eyes laid on the pools of blood on the stone ground. My jaw dropped open. I cupped my free hand over my mouth. Tori sheathed one dagger and stepped around the room. I stood in the doorway like a stunned mullet—my eyes wide and staring, and wet.

I was too late. I pushed myself too hard to escape that dungeon I was locked in with Levi. I shouldn't have gotten caught at all.

Tears streamed my face. My lungs tightened, and I gasped for air. Pain shot through my heart and soul. I collapsed to my knees, staring at the dark red. It was everywhere. My vision blurred, and I didn't bother to blink away the tears. He was gone.

Twenty

GONE.

I didn't have enough time with him. Somehow, I was in full control of my gift, even though this hurt worse than when I had lost Levi. Kill me now. Let them find me and kill me.

I fell forward onto my hands, allowing my head to bow down. My cheek found the cold stone, yet it didn't feel cold. I couldn't feel anything.

I closed my eyes. My skin was numb. My limbs were disconnected from my mind. But my heart ached. It was like fire burning through my veins.

When they find me, I hoped it would be quick. A stab to the temple or my heart to take this pain away. I didn't care anymore. I didn't want to live without him. He had become my everything over the past few months. *What was life without Kieran?* Nothing. It felt as though time had stopped. *Had time stopped?*

I drew my knees into my chest. Tears still flowed, pooling on the stone beside my cheek. My chest was hollow, yet somehow heavy. My breathing became shallow. *Was this the end?*

My muscles vibrated, yet I barely noticed. I ignored the pressure on my back and arm. *Had they found me?*

My friends. *Had my friends left and saved themselves?* I hoped they hadn't been caught too.

"Trixie."

My name reached my ears, but I shook my head. No. I'm imagining it.

"Trixie, come on."

Please, go away. Let me die here.

"Trix."

My nickname. Only Levi and Kieran called me Trix. Levi must be here. *Please, Levi, save yourself.*

My face rolled on the stone. A gripping pressure around my arm, rolling my body over. I refused to open my eyes. *Come on, kill me already.*

"Trix, it's me."

Yes, it was Levi talking to me. Not Kieran, because he

was…I couldn't even think of the word, even though I knew it to be true.

"Open your damn eyes." Levi demanded.

My arm shook under the pressure of his hand. He pushed against me roughly and pulled me up. My head hung. No. I didn't want to open my eyes. I didn't want to face the reality I already knew was true.

"Leave me to die." The words escaped my lips in a monotone sob.

"Never." Levi said. "He's not here. But he could still be alive."

No. Don't give me hope. Please, let me die.

"Trixie, you need to open your eyes." Jake's voice reached my ears. "I believe he's still alive. They would need him alive to bring you here."

What he said made sense, but I didn't want to believe it for my heart to be ripped out all over again.

"If you don't believe it, then fine." Tori stated. "Get revenge instead."

Revenge. Yes. My parents. My sister. They did this. They took away my childhood. They abandoned me. They caused my depression. They killed Kieran.

I snapped my eyes open and lifted my chin. Levi's face was close to mine. He released a breath, relief washing over his features. Levi pulled me into a tight, short-lived hug. He wrapped his arms around my waist and pulled me to my feet. I leant on him, my face soaked with tears.

"We will find him, I promise," Levi said, dragging a hand softly over my cheeks to wipe away the tears.

My face hardened. My eyes found Jake's.

"They will pay for this." I spat.

"Yes, they will." Jake's mouth quirked up at one side. "Together."

I nodded. "Together."

TORI WARPED THE stone walls and created paths for us to travel through. My mind, heart broken and torn, couldn't help her. The emptiness tormented my mind. The pool of blood filling my subconsciousness.

As we moved through the stone, the memories of Kieran being tortured in the visions swam clearly in front of me. Sienna's evil smirk and how she looked directly at me.

I shook myself, wiping a hand down my face as if wiping away the memory. They needed him alive for me to come here. I wasn't sure if that was comforting or not.

Tori spoke, cutting me out of my thoughts. "Everyone ready?"

Clara, Jake and Levi nodded, gripping their weapons tighter.

"Wait." I said.

They turned to face me, confusion written all over their faces.

"Just in case…you better put protection spells on to

stop me accidentally slowing you again." I looked at them sheepishly.

Jake smiled. "Good thinking."

"Hold the tunnel." Tori eyed me.

I nodded and focused on keeping our makeshift tunnel in place. "Got it," I said and a moment later I felt Tori's magic lift and I was holding it on my own.

Clara, Tori and Jake all placed their hands on their heads. Yellow magic snaked from Clara's fingertips over her. Tori's fingers enveloped herself in white. Jake's lime green magic licked at his fingers and covered his head.

The pressure from Tori's magic returned, and I locked eyes with her. She nodded, and I let go of my hold on the tunnel, relaxing from the power of the magic releasing.

Levi stared, his mouth half hanging open. My eyes flickered between him and my friends.

"Uh…this might be a stupid question." I shifted my feet. "Can you do that on Levi, too? Or just yourselves?"

"We can," Clara answered, stepping over to Levi.

Levi tensed. "What exactly does it do?"

"It's safe." Clara lifted her hand to either side of his face and he flinched. "It doesn't hurt."

Levi stared at her for a long moment and flickered his eyes to mine. The corners of my mouth lifted slightly, and I nodded encouragingly. He took a breath, his eyes returning to Clara.

"Okay." He said.

Yellow swirls erupted from her hands and engulfed

his face and head. Levi's hands clenched into fists, but he stayed still. When the magic dissolved away and he could see again, he stared wide-eyed across the space at me.

"Alright." Clara said, turning away from him.

I raised my eyebrows. "No pain, right?"

"No." He shook his head. "I've just never had magic used on me."

Jake clapped him on the shoulder. "Well, now you have."

"Let's move. I can't hold this forever." Tori muttered ahead of us.

Tori's strength with the warping was astounding. I couldn't imagine myself ever being as good as she was. Yet she believed my magic was stronger than hers. But magic always had its limits, and we were pushing them.

Levi moved next to Tori and showed her the gps.

"We should check in this area." Tori reached out and pointed to the screen.

He nodded. "I agree. If he wasn't in the dungeons, they must have him in the interrogation rooms."

Tori's head bobbed, and Jake joined her on the other side. He placed a hand on her lower back and looked over at the gps.

"We need to go up a floor." Jake said, then he, too, was pointing. "Take us to these stairs, and we can go up the stairs and into this room here."

"Yes, then we can warp through the walls to avoid

any patrols." Tori looked up at Jake, the same twinkle in her eyes from earlier.

Jake gazed back at her. "Sounds like a plan."

Tori swallowed and took a breath. Her eyes left Jake's, and he dropped his hand from her back. She pushed against the stone, clearing the path to the east, then turning south toward the staircase. She kept the stone surrounding us as we warped through rooms.

When we reached the staircase, she looked over her shoulder. "Ready?"

We all nodded, weapons in hands.

Tori opened up our stone protection, and the staircase stood in front of us. Like the dungeons, it was stone and covered in mould and dirt. Walls stood on either side, blocking us from view from anyone on the bottom floor.

Had anyone noticed the stone moving yet? Surely someone had already noticed the stone moving, and they had been alerted. *Would we be walking into an ambush?* I fiddled with Ivy in my grasp. Jake stepped into the stairwell, followed by Clara and I. We readied ourselves, watching the landing above and waiting for the space below us to be revealed.

Levi stepped out of the makeshift tunnel and Tori followed, releasing her hold on the stone. The stones moved back into the ground and walls to reveal a hallway which was vacant.

Empty. No Dark Soul Weavers waiting to attack us. No Sienna, nor my parents. I frowned. Jake and Clara exchanged wary glances. None of us dared speak. Clara's eyes glazed over. Jake's eyes became distance as he, too, opened up his senses. Clara shook her head and Jake gave her a thumbs up. No one was close by.

We stepped up the staircase slowly, keeping close to the walls. When we closed in on the above platform, Clara peered around the corner. Her hand waved us forward, and we followed her onto the second floor.

A hall spread out in both directions, stone like the rest of the castle. The hall to the right was short and turned to the south. Toward the left, the hall was longer and had several passageways and doors leading from it.

Jake pointed to Clara and Levi to go right. Jake, Tori and I headed left. Tori slipped her hand in her jacket and equipped herself with Ember. Jake lead the way quietly along the hall. We peered into the rooms and passageways as we went.

The first room was empty except for a table and chairs. Next, we had another empty room, smaller than the last, and nothing except for a single chair. Tori raised an eyebrow. Jake shook his head and turned to me. He pointed to me, then to his eyes, then to the hall behind us. I nodded in understanding and kept my eyes on the watch behind.

Levi and Clara had rounded the corner out of sight. I couldn't hear anything. I couldn't sense anyone nearby either. *Wait.* I couldn't sense Levi and Clara either.

My heart pounded hard in my chest. *Were they okay?*

I frowned and glanced over at Jake and Tori. They were peering into the passageway closest to us, then shifted toward the next door. I moved forward, keeping close to the wall, and glancing over my shoulder behind us to keep watch.

Why couldn't I sense Levi and Clara? My thumb rubbed over the hilt in my right hand. Something was wrong. They couldn't have moved that far away that we couldn't sense them. *Where had they gone?* Jake and Clara stood close together by the last door in the hall. But they stepped away from it. Another empty room.

Nervousness pulsed through my veins. *Where was Kieran?* I lifted my left hand and fiddled with the hem on my jacket. Something was definitely very wrong. I moved forward, constantly looking backward and down the passageway as I passed.

Jake and Tori reached the last passageway at the end of the hallway, and pressed themselves against the stone. Tori wrapped her hand around Jake's wrist and stood on her tippy toes to whisper in his ear. They were too far ahead for me to hear them, but they must sense the same uneasy feeling I had.

I stepped lightly along the hall, careful of where I stepped—tripping on the uneven stone floor was not an option. A crunch sounded from behind. I froze in place. Jake and Tori whipped their heads in my direction. I looked over my shoulder toward the sound.

Anticipation filled every single one of my muscles.

My pulse deafened me. My lungs expanded as I held a deep breath. I turned my back on Jake and Tori, eyes locked on the stairwell we had entered from.

Nothing followed the sound. My muscles relaxed, the pounding in my ears softening. I released the breath I had been holding and turned back to Jake and Tori. Their expressions had softened too, but their eyes widened a moment later and Jake threw up his arm.

I spun back around in time to see a Dark Soul Weaver staring at me. It wasn't just anyone, though. Pure white hair gelled up in spikes with wide emerald green eyes.

Twenty-One

DEMETRI'S UNREADABLE EXPRESSION did not change as he stared at us. His stance was confident and relaxed, unbothered by our sudden appearance, his eyes unblinking. The only sound was the beating of our own hearts, the silence around us suffocating as Demetri's gaze bore into us.

"Well, well, well." Demetri's voice drifted down the hallway. "Fancy seeing you three here."

His eyes darted between us before scanning our surroundings. My mouth felt dry and my breaths came in quick, shallow gasps. My heart raced, and I fixed my gaze upon his hands. He opened up his arms, and I raised my left palm toward him. Ivy's hilt remained gripped in my right hand.

"And where would Clara be?" his voice was different, sour.

"I was hoping you could tell us." I spat before Jake or Tori could answer.

His eyes locked on me, then drifted to the dagger in my hand. "Hmm, do you even know how to use that?"

Of course, he was going to avoid answering where they were. I don't know why I ever thought differently. There was a metallic taste in my mouth, like pennies, as I licked my lips.

"How long have you had this planned?" Jake asked.

Demetri's brow furrowed slightly as he pursed his lips, his eyes narrowing in concentration as he gazed at the ceiling. "Let's say, since I became head of the council."

I couldn't see the fury in Jake's eyes, but I could imagine it. They had trusted Demetri. He had led them for so many years and gave them no reason to doubt him. The sounds of heavy breathing and moans of disbelief and confusion filled the room.

"Ah, Tori. You were never supposed to come back. We hoped you had gone back to the magic-less world and would never return. One less nuisance to take care of, you know." Demetri stepped forward.

My left hand crackled, turquoise electricity escaping my fingertips. "No further." I snapped.

Demetri held up his hands in defence. "Okay, okay. Let's be civilised here."

"Civilised?" Tori said, with a half laugh. "You betrayed *everyone*."

"Yes, well, it was my task to keep everyone thinking I was on your side and Myrdreya was safe." He clicked his tongue. "It never was. Julianne was building up her forces to take Myrdreya, and I was helping her. It failed, of course, because Trixie was supposed to be on Julianne's side."

"And what of my father?" I asked in a low voice.

His lip curled. "Jay was to be accepted into Myrdreya, just as we had done, to assist me. We never planned on such a strong bond to be formed between you and Kieran."

My grip tightened on the dagger at the mention of Kieran's name. I ground my teeth, keeping my eyes focused on the man I had learned to trust. Kieran reported everything to Demetri, feeding him information that unknowingly aided the enemy.

"Kieran could have been spared if you hadn't bonded with him." Demetri continued, shaking his head. "Soul bonding is so rare and his soul had to choose you, didn't it?"

Soul Bonding. He didn't tell us before what it had been called. *If my soul was bound to Kieran's, why couldn't I feel him?* I hadn't felt him die. I hadn't felt his pain. I couldn't feel if he was alive, either.

"Of course." Jake muttered. "That's why your magic joined."

I swallowed. *Had I lost my soul mate before I could even start a life with him?* My gut churned. The pools of blood coming back to the front of my thoughts.

"But you can't feel him...can you?" Demetri said with the corner of his mouth lifting.

I blinked, staring directly into those emerald eyes. My brows furrowed as I studied his expression.

"What did you do?" Jake asked.

"Oh, it wasn't me." Demetri waved a hand. "Senses have been blocked so you can't sense anyone coming. It also means you can't sense your bonded soul, either."

"Where is he?" I said through gritted teeth.

Demetri shrugged. "Around here somewhere. He had been locked up in the dungeons until Sienna discovered you were coming."

"He's still alive?" I breathed.

"I think so. Maybe not for long, though." He smirked. "Sienna had some fun."

I clenched my jaw. I already knew what he was saying was the truth. Sienna would pay it—they all would.

"You knew all this time that I had a sister?" I asked.

He raised his eyebrows. "Yes. It was her plan to capture Kieran after you had left Myrdreya. We knew you would come to his rescue. And, look…here you are."

I didn't dare take my eyes off Demetri. Three against one. He wouldn't be stupid enough to attack us first unless we were distracted. His eyes flickered to the left for a split second, like he had heard something unseen.

I reached out for my senses, but there was nothing.

"What did you do to our senses?" I narrowed my eyes.

"Clever, isn't it?" Demetri smirked. "It's a gift of one of the Soul Weavers here. He can defuse the senses, to make us blind to them."

Clever was an understatement.

"Why?" Tori said, her voice stern. "Why betray us? We're family."

"Family?" Demetri laughed. "You are far from family."

"You've had this planned from the beginning." Jake said. "When Kieran landed on your doorstep, you were angry. You weren't angry that his parents died. You were angry that Kieran survived."

I sucked in a lung full of air.

Demetri's smirk widened. "Took you long enough. Although you weren't very good at your gift back then, otherwise you would have known."

"You traitor." Tori injected. "We gave everything to serve you, to follow you. And it's all been for a lie."

Demetri's voice was laced with sarcasm when he said, "sorry."

"My mother never killed your wife, did she?" I asked.

"No." His eyes darkened. "A mission that she had been on with Kieran's mother did. She left her to die. His mother left her to die."

I shook my head. "I don't believe that. If she did, she probably had no choice."

He threw his head back and let out a laugh that had no humour in it. "I pity you. Being bonded to Kieran. He will leave you to die like his mother did to my wife."

"So, he's definitely alive, then." I swallowed, ignoring his stab at Kieran's true allegiance.

"He'll die soon." He spat.

I flexed my outstretched hand and my knuckles on my right hand whitened as my fingers tightened around Ivy.

"Trixie." Tori called out. "You get the back."

You get the back. The back of what? What was she on about? Wait…it suddenly dawned on me.

"On you." I said back to her.

Demetri's brows furrowed as he glanced between us, his expression laced with confusion.

"NOW." Tori yelled.

I brought the stones up from the floor behind him. Tori pushed the stones up at the front.

"What the hell?" his eyes widened.

The stones blocked him from view, but we closed the walls around him, trapping him.

Liar.

Traitor.

Murderer.

I did not know what Tori's intentions were, but I knew what mine were. He tried to have Kieran killed with his parents when he was only a teenager. He played them all. Betrayed everyone who looked up to him. He organised Kieran's capture and allowed him to be tortured. He wasn't getting away with it.

I dropped my outstretched hand and stared hard at the stone. I barely noticed the panicked murmuring coming from behind the walls as I pushed the stone inwards. Although our senses were blocked, I could feel Demetri inside our warped chamber. He pushed against the stone, yelling for us to release him.

That was not on my agenda.

Bile rose into my throat and swallowed it back down. My heart pounding against my rib cage. I focused on Demetri and the stone surrounding him. A stone spike erupted and hit Tori's front wall. Another spike pierced into the wall, followed by a yelp from Demetri.

I vaguely heard his panicked voice through the thick stone. "Stop, please, let me out!"

No. There was no way I was letting him escape alive. A few more spikes erupted and pierced his flesh. A groan and more yelling followed. Ignoring his pleading, I pushed more spikes into his body.

"Trixie, what are you doing?" Tori's voice said beside me; when she had arrived at my side I hadn't noticed.

I shut her out. She would not stop me. Anger rolled through my muscles.

Demetri's body flattened against Tori's wall, several spikes holding him in place. He whimpered, but I could barely hear him. And I didn't care. I had no mercy. I pushed more spikes into his skin, hitting some vital organs. He gasped, no longer yelling or whimpering.

The stone rumbled in front of us. It shifted back toward the ground as Tori released her magic, revealing what I had done. Tori gasped and turned away. Jake hovered near us, staring at Demetri's impaled body. His head hung. Blood dripped from the wounds onto the floor.

"You killed him." Jake murmured.

The stone shifted. Spikes removed from his flesh and shrank back into the makeshift wall. Demetri's body collapsed onto the stone floor with a thud. The wall merged back into place like it had never been there.

I kept my eyes locked on Demetri's maimed body. I murdered him. I murdered a man. Blood drained from my face, my sweat turning cold. I didn't feel remorse for him. There was no regret in my heart, either. But the bile returned and there was no holding it in. I doubled over and what little food I had eaten smothered the stone floor.

A hand touched my back, rubbing circles.

"The first time is never easy." Jake said soothingly.

"We need to move." Tori's hollow voice reached my

ears as I straightened up. "Someone might have heard."

Careful not to look at Demetri again, I turned my back on him.

Twenty-Two

TRIXIE

WE ROUNDED THE CORNER, HEADING down the first corridor. Footsteps and surprised voices reached our ears from behind. Tori was right. They had heard.

Jake's hand gripped around my arm, and he pulled me into a nearby room. Tori closed the door quietly and beckoned us to follow her. The room was large, with a four-poster bed, an elegant but ancient wardrobe, and a powder desk with a mirror. Candles lined the walls, casting a dim lighting over the bedroom.

We stood in the far corner. Tori stepped forward in front of us. Stone warped up from the floor, blocking us from view.

A moment later, the door opened, and boots thudded on the floor. We held our breaths as the newcomer investigated the bedroom. After a few long moments, the footsteps grew further away.

"Clear." A man's voice announced and the bedroom door closed.

We released our breaths, and Tori waited a minute longer before releasing the wall. Jake checked the hall and indicated with his hand that we were in the clear.

My mind was distracted—I couldn't shake Demetri's bloodied body from it. I stepped forward, but my heavy legs felt like they weren't mine. I placed a hand over my queasy stomach.

"Let's go," Jake whispered.

Swallowing hard, I shook my head to remove the memory.

We stepped out of the bedroom and crept down the corridor. Jake and Tori checked each room we passed, and I followed along silently. Turning another corner, into another corridor, all the rooms here were empty too.

Kieran had to be here. He had to be alive. Demetri said he was. My heart dropped into the pot of my stomach. *What if he had been lying about that, too?* Giving me more hope for it to be ripped away even after Demetri's death. My face paled again, but only momentarily.

I gritted my teeth and lengthened my stride. Jake and Tori glanced at me curiously, and followed me back down the corridor we came. I lost Kiarra. I was not losing Kieran, too. He was still breathing. I knew it.

Scouting the corridor where Demetri had deceased—his body still laid in a pool of his blood—we marched down the hall, away from him, and peered around the corner. No one was in sight. We pushed forward, hurrying along the stone floor. The three of us opened doors one at a time and peered in.

Tori shook her head as we closed the 5th door. *Come on, Kieran. Where are you?* Having no extended senses really was similar to being blind—at least for Soul Weavers.

We opened the sixth door, Jake peering in. He shook his head; yet another empty room. My hope diminished quickly.

We turned to the last door in the corridor. The thumping in my chest beat faster. My breathing was heavy in my lungs. We crept forward and Jake gripped the handle. I bit my lip as he pulled the door open wide. We peered in.

Nothing.

Empty.

I breathed in sharply, backing away. Tori walked in and gazed around at the emptiness. Jake's eyes wandered back down the hall, but he didn't move. *This can't be right. He has to be here.* The air in my lungs tightened so much that it was painful. I swallowed and closed my eyes for a long moment.

When I reopened my eyes, Jake was pacing and Tori had re-emerged from the room. None of us spoke. Ivy was still gripped in my right hand. I clenched, unclenched, and re-clenched my fist around her hilt. I began pacing up and down the corridor, counting the doors as I sauntered.

One, two, three, four, five, six, seven.

One, two, three, four…

Five, six, seven…

I halted my pacing and stared at the wall opposite the seventh door. Looking over my shoulder, I glanced at each of the doors. They were all in sets—except the seventh room had no room opposite. I spun back to the blank stone wall. Reaching my left hand out, I touched the stone's cold, rough surface.

A presence stepped up beside me. Out of the corner of my eye, I glanced at Tori, who stared at the wall, too.

"There's only seven rooms." Tori muttered.

I nodded. "And a blank wall."

"Do you think…?" Tori didn't get to finish her sentence.

"HEY!" a voice yelled from the other end of the corridor.

We turned to face two Dark Soul Weavers standing side by side. A burgundy fireball blazed down the hall toward us. Jake wiped it out with a counter magic ball of his own.

"We'll sort them out," Tori said. "Trixie, you get that invisible door open."

More fireballs flew down the hall, but it was nothing Jake and Tori couldn't handle. I nodded and faced the stone wall. Frowning, I skimmed my left hand over its surface again, pushing to see if it would open. I stepped back half a metre and focused on warping the stone.

It wouldn't budge. I tried again.

Nothing.

"Anytime now." Jake said.

I shook my head and turned toward them. *Shit.* There was four Dark Soul Weavers now. One unconscious on the ground. They were moving closer and closer, trapping us in the corridor.

"It's not working." I stated, before throwing a turquoise ball down the corridor.

It narrowly missed my target, but hit another behind him. He fell sideways into the wall and groaned. He locked his eyes on me, smirking. Raising his hand, I glimpsed a cut across his palm. He threw a few fireballs at me — one straight after another. My mouth curled up at the corner and I watched as the balls froze in midair and the Dark Soul Weavers froze in place.

Their expressions changed from determination to horror. Jake and Tori glanced back at me for a split second before returning their attention to our attackers. One by one, they fell in slow motion as Jake and Tori let their magic loose upon them. I stepped out of the way of the fireballs coming toward me.

The stasis released, and the fireballs hit the stone wall behind and the bodies hit the floor.

"Not sure how long they'll be knocked out for," Tori said, walking over to me. "What happened? Why couldn't you just warp it open?"

I shook my head. "Something is blocking my gift. It wouldn't move."

Tori looked at the wall beside us, twisting her body toward it. After a long moment, she released a frustrated groan.

"What the hell?" Tori threw her arms up in the air.

"There must be another way to break in." Jake said, joining us at the wall. "The fact that neither of you can use magic against it means it must be blocking magic. There has to be a way in or they wouldn't be able to get in either."

"But, how?" I raised my eyebrows. "A stone pick?"

Tori scoffed.

"No, there is probably a certain type of magic." Jake answered, stepping closer to the wall.

"Great." I huffed. "How are we going to get in? He must be in there if they've protected it this much."

Jake nodded. "I agree. I think we've found him."

I glanced down the corridor at the man that had focused his attacks on me. Leaving Jake and Tori by the wall, I walked over to his limp body. His eyes were wide and staring. He focused on me and watched as I crouched down next to him. I picked up his hand, facing the palm up, and eyed the cut. It was fresh, but not bleeding.

I narrowed my eyes on his face for a moment before letting his hand drop. I knew how to open the hidden room. My heart raced, and I hurried back to the wall. I raised Ivy to my palm.

"Wow." Tori grasped my wrist. "What are you doing?"

"What type of magic can ancient wielders do?" I asked.

Tori frowned. "A lot of different types. Create things out of thin air. Some could summon fire or water out of nothing. Others turned dark and used blood magic."

"Blood magic." I repeated. "It's a blood lock."

"Are you sure?" Tori asked.

I nodded, pointing to the unmoving man. "He has a cut on his palm and it's not bleeding."

Tori released my wrist. "At least let me do it."

"No." Jake said. "You're not tainting your blood to blood magic."

Tori looked into Jake's eyes. Before either of us could stop him, he pulled out a small dagger and pressed it to his palm. A thin slice, a small trickle of blood, and he raised his hand and pressed it to the surface of the stone.

The stone immediately melted away, revealing a small room, and it wasn't empty.

Twenty-Three

TRIXIE

SHACKLED BY HIS WRISTS FROM the high ceiling was Kieran. Blood dripped from his skin where the bindings dug in. His body was battered and worse than I had seen in my visions. *Had he eaten?* His stomach appeared sunken in. His head hung, his fringe covering his eyes. Blood covered his cheek. Covered from head to toe in dirt, wounds, blood, and…

I gasped.

What happened to his chest? I strode forward and stopped inches from him. My eyes widened, staring at the burns on his chest. Heart racing, I held my breath as I watched his chest. When it slowly rose and fell, I released my breath.

"He's a-alive." My voice shook, and I glanced over my shoulder at Tori and Jake.

Jake's tense shoulders slumped, and Tori sighed in relief. I turned back to Kieran and reached my hand up, placing it gently on his shoulder.

"Kieran?" I whispered, tears welling in my eyes.

Jake sauntered around the room, looking over Kieran's body and glancing out the small window to the north-east. I ducked my head down, looking up at Kieran's face.

"We're here." I said, rubbing my hand down his arm. "Can you hear me?"

Kieran took a deep breath and cracked his mouth. He let out a soft moan, and I whimpered, tears falling down my cheeks. The agony from his wounds traumatised me. I blinked rapidly, the wetness spilling over. I wiped my cheeks with the back of my hand.

"We're going to get you out of here." I eyed the metal locked around his wrists. "Jake, can you support him?"

Jake nodded and stood on Kieran's other side.

He paused for a moment, staring at Kieran's face. Saying nothing, he put his arm around Kieran's waist and held onto him.

"Okay." Jake said. "When you're ready."

I swallowed and focused on the shackles. My pulse

deafened me. *I can do this.* I took a deep breath and released it slowly. I reached up to hold his arms from falling. Carefully, I focused on the metal thinning and stretching. For a moment, I thought my magic was still blocked in this room, but then it followed my instructions.

The metal stretched, releasing Kieran's wrists. He grunted as his body slumped, but Jake had a good grip on him. His arms dropped. I gripped them tighter and guided them down, looping his right arm around Jake's shoulders. I allowed his other arm to rest beside his beaten bodice.

"We've got you," Jake said.

Kieran planted his feet on the ground, breathing heavily like his chest had been released from the bounds of a corset. He blinked his eyes open, taking a few moments to gain focus.

I brushed a hand over the left side of his face, moving dirt and blood to inspect the damage. Kieran flinched away from my hand, but then relaxed. I ran my fingers through his fringe and pushed it back. I lifted his chin to face me, revealing the horror of the right side of his face.

I gasped. "What did she do to you?"

"Fire. Burns." He muttered and pulled his face away from me.

He shrank back into Jake, avoiding my gaze.

"Please, don't look at me." He said.

My heart broke. He was ashamed. Ashamed of what

had happened. Ashamed of me seeing him torn like this.

I placed my hand on his left cheek. "Don't hide from me. No matter what you look like, I'll still love you."

He hesitated, glancing sideways at me.

"Kieran, please." I tilted my head toward him. "I love you no matter what. Please, show me."

He turned his face toward me after what felt like an eternity. Sadness haunted his eyes. I gave him an encouraging smile and moved my eyes over the burn. She hadn't touched his eye or ear, but burned the side of his face from the hairline to his jaw.

My jaw flexed, and I ground my teeth. I adverted my eyes to his chest. A clear hand print had burned into his flesh. The burn had looked so fresh minutes ago, but now it was…healing?

"How deep does this go?" I asked, frowning.

"To my ribs, I think." Kieran answered, his voice clearer than it had been. "It's more numb than anything now."

"But, how? You should still be in agony."

He shook his head. "I don't know."

"We've got company." Tori whispered. "Footsteps coming. Two, I think."

"Can you stand?" I asked Kieran.

"I think so," he said, unwrapping his arm from Jake's shoulder.

Jake slowly released his arm from around Kieran's waist. Kieran toppled sideways and Jake caught him around the waist again.

"I'm alright." Kieran said, waving Jake away.

I bit my lip as Jake released him again, but hovered closely. Kieran took a couple of steps and lent against the wall.

"They're coming." Tori whispered.

Kieran nodded and pointed toward the doorway. Jake and I joined Tori and waited.

"I still can't sense anything." I whispered.

"It's a gift." Kieran whispered. "That's how they captured me."

There was a groan in the hallway, a flash of yellow and a thump. We looked at each other. I frowned. Tori carefully peered around the wall. She sighed and stepped out into the hall. Jake and I followed. I glanced back at Kieran—he was leaning his shoulder against the wall, watching us.

"About time." Tori said.

"Sorry, we got held up." Clara said, her ponytail bobbing as she hurried toward us. "Did you find him?"

We nodded. There was a movement to the left of where Clara stood, and she turned and threw a yellow fireball before he could even sit up. Levi had blood down his left arm.

He caught me looking at it and said. "Don't worry, it's not mine."

I nodded and looked at Clara. "You're both unhurt?"

"Yes, we're fine." Clara said. "How's Kieran?"

My face paled, and my stomach clenched. Clara looked between each of us.

"He's not…"

"No, he's alive." Jake answered, inclining his head to toward the room. "In here."

We lead them to the room. I crossed the space and allowed Kieran to slip his arm around my shoulders. Half for support, and half for the closeness we both missed.

Clara gasped and shook her head. "Okay, you've got to fill us in later. But now, let's get out of here."

"No." I retorted, and every pair of eyes was on me. "I am *sick* of running from them. I am *sick* of hiding. I will *not* let them take anything else from me."

Kieran smiled weakly at me. *How was he still so handsome, even covered in dirt, blood and burns?* Because I loved him. No matter how he looked, I wanted him. I rested my forehead against his.

"Demetri, h-he…" Kieran stumbled on his words.

"He's dead." Jake said bluntly. "And we know what he did. He lied about everything."

Kieran nodded. "He betrayed us."

"Demetri and my family took your parents away from you. Now I will kill them for you, for us." I whispered.

"Are you sure?" he croaked.

I nodded. "With every beat of my heart."

"I'm with you." Levi said, stepping forward.

I glanced over at him, straightening up my posture. Kieran shifted beside me and I could feel his eyes on me.

"We're all with you." Jake said.

I eyed each one of them. Clara nodded at me. Tori gave me a half smile. Jake lifted his chin.

"Thank you." I closed my eyes momentarily before glancing back to Kieran. "I think you need to get out of here, though."

Kieran glared at me. "Never. I go where you go."

"But—."

"You are everything to me. I will not let you go against your family without me." He said, holding my hands in his. "Besides, I'm healing quicker than expected. Look…"

He turned his chest for everyone to view the burns. He was right. The burns weren't flaming red anymore; they were lightening in colour. We all gaped at him.

"How—?" I began.

"Your gift." Jake mumbled, and I frowned at him.

Kieran smiled at his best friend. "I think…I think it's back."

I looked between them, raising my eyebrows. "Someone want to explain?"

"He lost his gift." Clara said.

"I thought you didn't have one." I frowned.

"I used to. But a Dark Soul Weaver cursed me with ancient magic. My gift disappeared." Kieran explained, his voice cracking. "I thought it was gone for good."

"How is that possible?" I gaped at him. "I didn't know magic could even be taken away."

Kieran looked away for a long moment. "Neither did I. But I didn't think it could return either."

"So, you can heal?" I asked. "You have the ability to self-heal."

He shook his head. "Not just self-heal. I can heal others too, but it has its limitations. I can't save someone from the brink of death."

"That's...incredible." I stepped closer to him, tightening my hold on his hands. "How long will it take for you to heal yourself?"

"I'll heal mostly within the hour, but the scars..." he hesitated, averting his eyes from me, "they will remain."

I freed my hand from his grasp and placed it on his chin, turning him to face me. I eyed the burns on his face—now appearing to be a week old. Leaning in, I planted a soft kiss on his burnt cheek. When I pulled away, Kieran eyed me, his expression unreadable.

"Your scars are as handsome as you." I whispered.

His mouth was on mine. I could taste dirt and blood, but I didn't care. His arms wrapped and tightened around me, holding my body against his. His body folded against mine, and I entwined my fingers into his disheveled hair.

"Alright, lovebirds." Jake cleared his throat. "We gotta get moving if we want to catch three Dark Soul Weavers."

I reluctantly pulled away, Kieran planting one more kiss on my lips before we allowed our attention to focus on Jake. Jake shimmied out of his jacket and handed it to Kieran. Kieran looked down at himself; it was like it was the first time he realised he was wearing nothing but boxers. He took the jacket and pulled it up his arms and over his back.

"Let's do this," Kieran said, fastening the zipper on the jacket.

I nodded. "Let's do this."

Twenty-Four

HEARING TRIXIE'S VOICE WAS BOTH a relief and a disappointment. She'd walked right into their trap with coming here. But if she hadn't, I would still be shackled and slowly bleeding to death. I was supposed to save her—not the other way around.

Her soothing voice in my ears sent dread through my body. I didn't want her to meet the same fate. Her eyes filled with sadness and pity when she saw the burns on my face. *How would anyone love someone so scarred?*

Ashamed, I couldn't look at her.

Tori and Trixie warped us through the castle. Trixie's eyes continuously flickering to me, checking I was alright. My burns were healing faster than I could have hoped for. My balance had returned and I could walk on my own. Feelings of helplessness and self doubt evaporated the further we moved through the black castle.

They created stairs, and we moved up to the third floor. We could hear surprised voices behind the walls and we knew when we emerged, they would be waiting.

"Be ready for anything." Clara whispered, gripping her dagger in her right hand.

"The moment the wall opens up, they will be on us," Tori whispered over her shoulder. "Don't hesitate."

I touched Trixie softly on her arm, my lips close to her ear. "Are you sure you're ready for this?"

Trixie squeezed my hand, her gaze locking with mine. "I've never been more ready."

Levi readied his sword in front of his body. Jake stepped in front of him, his back toward Levi.

"Stay behind us when they unleash their magic." Jake whispered over his shoulder. "Metal isn't a shield."

Levi nodded, keeping himself behind Jake's body. Clara held up her left hand and gripped her dagger in her right. Tori pulled Ember from her jacket and held it tightly in her left hand. Jake tucked his hand into his pant pocket and pulled out a dagger, handing it to me.

I gave him a quick nod, taking the dagger and unsheathing it. I slipped the sheath into the inner pocket of Jake's jacket and weighed the dagger in my right hand. Inspecting the small blade, I poked my pinky finger in the ring at the end of the hilt. I flicked it around in a circle, catching the hilt in my palm—a perfectly balanced Karambit dagger.

"Shadowbite." Jake whispered.

I nodded. I had seen Jake wield Shadowbite before, of course. But I had never actually known its name.

I flexed my jaw, testing the extension of the burn on my cheek. It grew tight—I ran my fingertips over the scar tissue. Taking a deep breath, the air flowed through my lungs with ease. The skin tightened on my chest beneath the jacket.

"Ready?" Tori twisted her body toward us all.

I dropped my hand away from my face. We all nodded in unison and gripped our weapons tighter.

"When the wall drops, so do we," Tori whispered.

Tori and Trixie locked gazes for a split second before giving each other a curt nod. The grey stone crumbled away, revealing a large open plan room with high ceilings, lit with candles.

A dozen Dark Soul Weavers stood in a circle surrounding us. Multiple colours lit up in their palms—fireballs flying toward us. Simultaneously, we dropped to the stone floor. An array of colours burst above us. Showering us with magical sparks. Those fireballs that didn't hit others flew across the room and hit a few Dark Soul Weavers.

Nine still stood around us. We rolled and jumped to our feet. Levi stood inside our loose circle. Trixie stood on my right, Jake on my left. We each faced one or two Dark Soul Weavers dressed in black and red—none of them were Trixie's family.

The man with the ponytail and oak eyes smirked at me. *Asshole*. I gritted my teeth. His hand raised up, but I released my violet magic before he could strike. He spun sideways and easily avoided my fireball. He threw a magenta ball back toward me and I countered it with a ball of my own—obliterating it into pieces.

"Did you get the short end of the straw?" I mocked. "Pink magic."

He clenched his jaw, fury in his eyes. I smirked.

"Come on, show me what you got." I taunted, keeping my eyes locked on him as I stepped toward him.

"What happened to your face?" the man snickered. "It looks like half of you is now a shrivelled apple."

"I think it makes me look daring." I said. "Maybe you should ask her to burn your face. It would certainly be an improvement."

He brought both hands up, his palms filling with magenta. As he released the magic toward me, I ducked, somersaulted and jumped up in front of him. My fist cracked him in the jaw, knocking his head backward. He stumbled and shook off the shock of the blow.

He swung a right hook toward my head. I ducked and jabbed Shadowbite at his side. He curled his body out of reach, but the blade caught him on the forearm. The curved metal carved a deep wound and blood dripped onto the stone. A hiss escaped the man's lips, and he cupped a hand over the gash.

My mouth curled up at the corner, and I slashed toward him again with the sharp blade. Shadowbite collided with flesh, tearing a gaping hole in his waist. The man gasped and clutched at his side, red seeping through his fingers.

"Not so tough now, are you?" I said, Shadowbite clutched in my hand, in front of my chest, dripping with blood.

A body fell to the stone floor metres away. I tore my eyes away, scouting for Trixie. She stood close to where she started, panting. Ivy held tightly in her grasp, the blade red. A woman with red hair in a pool of blood at her feet, unmoving. Delaras.

Trixie's eyes met mine and her beautiful mouth curled. Her smile was short-lived as her expression changed, her eyes widening. Something hard and sticky collided with my body, knocking me to the ground. My right arm crushed under the weight and my face smashed against the stone.

Hands held me on the cold floor. I twisted and glimpsed the bloody gash in his forearm—dripping onto my skin.

"Not so tough now…" he leaned in, repeating my own words, "are you?"

I groaned against his weight, shifting in an attempt to push him off. Out of the corner of my eye, turquoise exploded in the man's face and the pressure immediately disappeared. I rolled over and pushed myself off the ground. Trixie stood over the man on the ground, her dagger at his throat.

"Are you wishing you didn't do that now?" she hissed at him.

He stared up at her, smirking. "You don't have the heart. You wouldn't—." His voice cut off, and he choked. His eyes widened and blood poured from the slit in his throat.

"I would." Trixie snapped, wiping her blade on his clothes.

She straightened up, and we both turned to the others. We watched as a Dark Soul Weaver fell at Jake's feet. A body sat at the base of the opposite wall, a trail of blood visible where he had slid down it. Another lay unmoving a metre away from it.

Clara ripped her dagger from the chest of a Dark Soul Weaver. Their scream turned into a gurgle as their mouth filled with blood and spilled over their chin. The body collapsed to the ground.

I scouted the room.

All the Dark Soul Weavers were dead in their own blood. Jake had a minor cut on his leg, the blood soaking his black gear. Clara and Tori looked unscathed.

Trixie moved to my side. Her hand slipped into mine and she eyed me over. I glanced over at her—she appeared unharmed.

"Are you okay?" Trixie squeezed my hand.

I nodded, kissing her lightly on her forehead. "Twelve down."

I placed my arm around her waist and held her up against me. It was still surreal that she was here.

"Aw, isn't that just touching?" A familiar voice echoed through the room.

We all turned and watched Julianne striding in, with Sienna and Jay on her heels.

Julianne's lips curled, her eyes locked on Trixie and I. "Souls united."

Twenty-Five

TRIXIE

MY HEART LEAPT INTO MY throat. My mysterious secret sister, maleficent mother, and traitorous father all had their eyes on Kieran and I. I reluctantly released Kieran from my embrace and turned my body toward my disowned family. My parents no longer deserved to be called my parents—in fact, they lost that title the moment they betrayed me.

"Hello daughter." Julianne said, her arms opening up wide as if I would run to her for a hug. "It's so nice of you to join us."

I levelled her with a glare. Nice was not what this was. I kept my focus on Sienna and my mother.

"I see you found him." Sienna sniggered. "Interesting that your burns are already so healed."

"You made a mistake." I whispered loud enough for them to hear.

Sienna's eyebrow raised. "What was that?"

I stared directly into her eyes. "I said *you* made a mistake."

"I don't think so." She pursed her lips.

Jay shifted. "Trixie-pix—."

"Shut up." I snapped at Jay. "How dare you?"

Jay lifted his chin but kept his mouth closed.

I eyed him with a dirty expression before turning my eyes back on Sienna. Julianne and Jay may have murdered Kieran's parents, but Sienna had attacked and almost killed Kieran. It wasn't happening again.

Turquoise sparked at my fingertips.

"Tut tut, now let's not be hasty." Julianne said, shaking her head at me.

"You took everything from me. You took my childhood. You took my life. You took Kieran's parents. And you almost took Kieran." I said through gritted teeth.

"Don't forget we took Kieran's healing gift as well." Sienna clicked her tongue.

I glanced sideways at Kieran.

He stared at Sienna, frowning.

"It was you." Kieran mumbled.

Sienna's smirk grew wider. "Yes, it was *me*."

His fist clenched at his side, and I reached my hand out, cupping his hand. He flexed and allowed me to take his hand in mine.

"Alright, enough of this." Julianne's voice boomed around the room. "Trixie, hand yourself over and the others can go free."

"What do you want with her?" Tori asked.

Jake was standing near Tori, protectively. His hand in hers.

"We just want our family complete again." Jay voiced.

I scoffed. All heads turned to me.

"Family?" I spat. "You don't know the meaning of it. You're *not* my family."

"I'm pretty sure I birthed you." Julianne said, raising her brows.

I laughed. "And that makes you my family? No. You lost that right. Family doesn't have to be blood. I have a real family."

I stepped closer to Kieran and indicated to Tori, Jake, Clara and Levi with my free hand.

Julianne's nostrils flared. "You're our family. You will see."

"Why?" I asked. "Why did you do all of this?"

"We were supposed to take Zalindor as a family."

Julianne said. "My two daughters joining their magic together and creating something beautiful and lethal."

I frowned, looking between Julianne and Sienna. They only wanted power. *Of course they did.*

"You abandoned me as a child because I showed no power." I said. "So, I was useless to you. Then you discovered I wasn't just a useless human. Demetri fed you all the information you needed."

"Yes, he was useful. Pity you killed him." Julianne said, with no remorse in her tone.

Kieran frowned, glancing at me. *Oh, yeah, we didn't tell him who had actually killed him.* I wasn't even sure how Julianne knew I had done it.

"Yes, I killed him." I breathed, gripping Ivy tighter. "And he deserved it."

Sienna's mouth curled. Julianne's pursed.

"I say we stop this chatter and get to what we all want to do right now," Levi said, flipping his sword in his hand.

"I almost didn't see you there, Levi." Julianne said. "But, I agree. It's time you turn your sword on your pretend friends."

Levi laughed. Jake eyed Levi, his hand slowly moving to his own sword.

"They are my *real* friends." Levi swallowed, eyeing Jake's subtle movement.

Jake narrowed his eyes, focusing on Levi for a long moment. He lifted his chin after a moment, relaxing and turning his gaze back to my traitorous family. I released a breath slowly.

"Okay, I'm done with this." Tori sidestepped from Jake and stared ahead.

The stone rumbled under Julianne's, Jay's, and Sienna's feet. They eyed me, but I shook my head and pointed at Tori. Their eyes widened, and they glanced at each other when realisation overcame them. They moved quickly, avoiding the tidal wave of stone threatening to throw them into the air or bowl them over.

A rainbow of colours burst around the room as fireballs released from our hands. Levi ducked and weaved away from the chaos of colour. Tori formed spikes from the ground, but they were always a step ahead of her.

Yelling reached our ears from the doorway my ex-family had entered through. Two Dark Soul Weavers joined the explosion of colours. Tori and Jake turned their focus on them as they threw fireballs toward Levi.

I took my focus off Tori and Jake and formed stone fencing around my father, separating him from Julianne and Sienna. Kieran threw fireballs defensively at Julianne and Sienna, stopping their magic from reaching us. Levi ran across the room toward Jay with his sword out, his target in sight.

He glanced at me, and I gave him a quick nod. My eyes turning back to Jay, I wrapped the stone around his ankles and arms. He stared at me, eyes wide.

"Trix —." Jay's voice cut short, and he adverted his gaze.

I followed his line of sight to his chest where Levi's sword had hit home through his ribs. He gasped, failing to suck in air. Blood poured from his chest and gurgled out his mouth. I released the stone and his body collapsed.

Levi leaned down, placing two fingers at Jay's neck. His eyes met mine, and he nodded. I kept my expression blank — no sadness and no relief. Jay was dead. My father was dead. One down, two to go.

To my left, Kieran kept Julianne and Sienna at bay. Neither of them noticed Jay had fallen. Sienna scowled as a purple fireball grazed her arm. Julianne's white magic burst in the air above and rained down a multitude of tiny balls.

My eyes widened, and I gasped. Kieran bolted backward, narrowly missing the shower and almost colliding into me.

A scream sounded through the room and we all faced the direction it came from. A stone spike as thick as a branch impaled one of the Dark Soul Weavers. From the moment of distraction, a whimper reached my ears, and I turned.

Levi's eyes found mine. His mouth hung open and the light in his eyes paled. I gaped at the metal sticking out of his stomach. He fell to his knees as someone ripped the sword back out of his body. Another Dark

Soul Weaver stood behind him, his eyes on the back of Levi's head.

Ivy clattered to the stone ground, and my scream echoed around the room. "LEVI!"

Half a dozen Dark Soul Weavers entered the room and lined the walls near the doorway. Seeing them in my peripheral vision, I didn't take my eyes off Levi. My muscles wouldn't obey me. I couldn't move.

The man thrust the sword back into his body again and twisted. The air rushed out of my lungs as it did Levi's. His eyes grew heavy, a single tear falling from the corner of his eye.

"Kill…them." Levi said soundlessly, and he buckled over, his body hitting the floor.

The sword dripped with blood and the man's gaze turned to me with a malicious grin, his crooked teeth showing.

At that moment time stopped. All the Dark Soul Weavers, except Julianne and Sienna, froze. My heart split open all over again. A million pieces shattering through my body.

And I wailed.

My arms opened wide and my head fell back—I screamed. The pitch was deafening. If there were windows in the room, the glass would have shattered. Gasps and groans filled the surrounding air.

I dropped my head and stared straight ahead. Spikes sprouted from the walls, impaling all the Dark Soul

Weavers lining it. Blood dripped from their bodies and mouths.

Tori, Jake and Clara clustered together with spikes surrounding them. Tori's eyes were locked on mine. Fear flowed through my veins. I eyed their bodies, but they were unharmed. Tori must have blocked the stone from harming them.

I released a gush of air and turned to Kieran, who stood close behind me. The stone hadn't moved near us and behind us. I stepped away from him, holding my hands up.

"Trix, I'm okay." Kieran hushed.

"I-I just…" my voice shook, fear rooting me in place.

"It's alright, you didn't hurt us." He said.

I shook my head. "Please, stay back."

"Don't do this," Kieran said, his eyes widened. "Please, Trix, do not shut me out."

The spikes released, and the bodies slumbered to the stone ground. I flickered my gaze to Tori and Jake. They both stared back at me.

"You had a lot of emotions built up inside you." Tori explained. "You just released it. Don't be scared."

Kieran held out his hand, and I glanced down at it for a moment. I reached out and took his hand. He stepped forward and drew me close.

"You're okay." He whispered, before drawing away and looking across the room behind us.

I twisted and looked over my shoulder. Julianne and

Sienna stared wide-eyed at me. For a moment, I thought I had frozen them in place, but then they both turned and ran out a doorway to the left.

"NO!" I yelled and bolted after them.

I heard footsteps behind me and the voices of Tori, Jake, and Clara in the distance. Kieran and I rounded the corner through the door and strode along the hallway. Fire blazed behind us. We turned to find the doorway blocked and Tori, Jake and Clara shouted through the flames.

"And now there were two." Julianne cackled, and we turned our backs on the fire.

A white fireball flew toward us, and we separated, dodging its impact. Another came immediately after and hit Kieran in the arm. He threw a purple ball back down the hall toward Julianne.

Sienna sidestepped into a room off the hall, her cruel gaze locking on me before she disappeared. Julianne and Kieran continued throwing fireballs at one another. I bolted down the hall and dived into the room after Sienna.

"TRIXIE!" Kieran yelled behind me.

I paused inside the doorway. Sienna had her back turned toward me. She twisted and glanced over her shoulder.

"Hello, sister." Her face twisted, and she stepped to the right.

I moved further into the room, stepping to the left.

"Isn't it nice to spend some quality time together?" Sienna continued circling the room, and I moved left to keep myself on the opposite side from her.

Flames rose in the doorway, blocking us from any escape. The mumbling from Kieran and Julianne drifted in, but faint.

"I have no sister." I scowled.

Sienna pouted. "Aw, come on, don't be like that."

"Until a few days ago, I didn't know you existed."

"Oh, but you met me when I blew up that house." She heaved a sigh. "That family probably got a shock when they came home."

"We thought you died." I swallowed. "How did you even survive that explosion?"

"Well, you see, it was all set up. You weren't supposed to be able to escape...but, you surprised me with your magic shield."

The vision of Kieran's magic and my magic combining floated into my mind briefly before the flesh wounds on Kieran's body took over.

"You burnt him," my nostrils flared.

Her mouth curled. "Yes, doesn't he look...menacing?"

"You almost killed him." I snapped.

"Aw, don't be so angry. I think it's an improvement. And, look, he survived...for now." Her smile twisted.

I raised my hand and threw a turquoise fireball at her face. She ducked easily away from it, laughing. *Laughing.*

How dare she? My blood boiled, and I ground my teeth.

"You're psychotic."

She pouted. "No, I'm powerful. I've got more power than you can ever imagine."

"What do you want with me, then?" my pulse hammered in my ears.

"Your magic." She smirked. "And I will take every ounce."

I frowned. She had moved closer, and I hadn't noticed until now that she was only a metre away. My heart pounded so hard in my chest and my lungs tightened. Sienna's demeanour turned savage and her expression wrathful.

Flames grew from the floor up behind me. The heat bore into my back and I jumped a few inches forward.

Sienna chuckled. "Don't worry…it won't take long. You can go back to your normal human life."

I swallowed, glaring at her. *Alright, enough of this.* I raised my hand, turquoise sparking, but Sienna batted my hand away and thrust her other hand into my throat. My hands flew up and gripped her wrist. She squeezed my throat, and I gasped for air. Her free hand touched my chest, and she stared into my eyes.

A shiver crawled down my neck like thousands of spiders running over my skin. Searing pain rippled through my bones. My eyes flew wide. If I could breathe, a scream would have escaped my lips.

No. I can't die like this. Kieran, please. Please, someone help me. I couldn't take my eyes off Sienna's. Her expression was determined. She didn't blink. She didn't speak. She stared at me as she drained away my magic. As quickly as I learnt I had magic, she was taking it away.

My eyes grew heavy. My lungs were out of air. *Was she going to kill me, after all?* My new life, where I had found peace with myself, being ripped away from me. A waterfall of tears flowed down my cheeks. My airways burned raw from no oxygen. My eyes fluttered closed.

A scream reached my ears. The pressure from my throat disappeared and my body collapsed.

Twenty-Six

KIERAN

TORI, JAKE, AND CLARA JUMPED through the flames behind. Yellow, green, and white fireballs flew past me. Julianne's eyes widened, and she screamed. Upon impact, she fell to the stone. I bounded forward with Shadowbite.

Julianne shifted, and I didn't hesitate. I jabbed the blade into her neck. She gasped, her hands reaching for Jake's jacket I wore and clenching a fist full of leather.

"That is for my parents." I spat.

I pulled the dagger from her neck, and flexing my

jaw, I stabbed again.

"And that is for Trixie."

Her neck and shoulder dowsed in red as her body slumped. Her eyes faded and her hands dropped.

Ripping the dagger from her flesh again, her dead body thumped to the ground. I breathed hard, staring down at her body.

"Where is Trixie?" Tori asked.

Before I answered, Sienna stepped out of the room she had disappeared with Trixie in. My heart sank, and I stood.

Sienna eyed her dead mother, her jaw slack. She shrieked and her hand flew up.

Something gripped the back of my jacket and pulled me sideways into another room to the left. I turned as Jake released me and Tori sealed the doorway shut with stone.

"Where is she?" Tori asked again.

I shook my head. "Sienna. She exited that room. Trix…"

"Trixie was in that room with her?" Clara asked.

I nodded, my heart pounding behind my ribs. I lost her. After everything, I had lost her. I put my hands in my hair, gripping fistfuls.

Tori walked over to the wall toward the room Trixie and Sienna had been in. The stone shifted, and an archway formed, opening up into the other room.

I gasped and bolted through it. Trixie laid on the

ground unconscious. They followed me into the room. Gritting my teeth, I turned. The stone in the archway had already returned to its natural form. I started toward the doorway and Tori closed it off.

"What are you doing?" I growled. "We have to go after her!"

"Tend to Trixie first. You can heal her." Tori said.

I shook my head. "I c-can't"

"Yes, you can," Tori stated, pointing at Trixie.

I glanced down at her, my brows furrowed. I bent down and placed my hand on her face. A pulse in her neck was barely visible, but her chest was rising. Kneeling beside her, I lifted her head and placed it in my lap. With one hand on her cheek and the other on her chest, I closed my eyes.

I sucked in a lung full, holding it in for a few seconds before slowly releasing it. Her heart beat under my palm and my own hammered in my ears. *I can't lose her. I love her. She's everything to me. Don't leave me, Trixie. Come back to me.*

The breathing of my friends reached my ears. The screams from Sienna penetrated the stone walls Tori held up. Her fury was evident in her voice. Ignoring the surrounding sounds, I refocused on Trixie's breathing and heartbeat. Taking another breath, I pushed my magic into her body.

My hand tingled. Purple light filtered through my eyelids—the glow from my magic. *Come back to me, Trixie.*

I can't live without you. I'm nothing without you. My fingertips grew warm and became numb. The light grew stronger and threatened to blind me, even with my eyes closed.

Minutes passed. My magic faded, the purple glow disappearing. Chest tight, my heart thumping behind my ribs.

Trixie gasped.

I released the air in a whoosh from my lungs and snapped my eyes open. Looking down, Trixie's eyes were open and staring up at me.

I shifted and pulled her up to my chest. "Trix."

She panted, wrapping her arms around me. Holding her tightly, I pressed my lips on the top of her head.

"I thought I lost you." I whispered.

She mumbled into my chest. "I'm okay. I'm here."

"Are you able to stand?" Tori asked.

Trixie nodded and seated herself upright. "I think so."

"Take it slow." I said.

She pushed up off the ground and I supported her around the waist as she steadied herself on her feet. Her gaze brushed over us, clearly checking we were all here. Her blank expression and a single tear dripping from her eye told me her memory of Levi's death was intact.

"Julianne?" Trixie asked, her head turning to me.

I averted my eyes for a split second before looking directly at her. "Dead."

She nodded once.

"Where's Sienna?" Her voice was strong and fierce.

An angry shriek behind the walls answered her question for us. Her eyes locked on the direction Sienna's scream came from.

"She's mine." She said through gritted teeth.

Twenty-Seven

SIENNA WAS MINE. Levi killed my father. Kieran killed my mother. Sienna was mine.

"Are you sure you're ready for this?" Kieran intertwined his fingers with mine.

I stepped closer to him. "As long as you're with me."

"I'm right here with you," his lips pressed against mine.

"We will defend you." Clara said.

I reluctantly pulled away from Kieran and looked over at my friends. Jake nodded, and Tori smiled.

"You can't stay in there forever!" Sienna's voice trailed through the stone.

"Ready?" Tori asked.

Taking a quick breath, I said, "let's get her."

"We'll get back to the large room. She will follow us there. I'll hold the doorways shut so she can't escape. Jake, Clara, Kieran, you stop her magic touching Trixie." Tori turned to me. "Then it's up to you."

We nodded. Tori turned to the stone, and it started warping. We all faced toward the shifting stone as it became a tunnel. We traveled through in under a minute, encased in the stone. Tori opened a small window now and then to get her bearings, as we didn't have Levi's gps.

"REALLY?" Sienna yelled. "YOU'RE GOING TO KEEP HIDING?"

Tori was right. She followed us. I nodded to Tori, and she released the stone.

The stone walls melted away into the surrounding floor. Sienna stood metres away, a wicked grin crossing her face. Her expression changed abruptly when she spotted me.

"So, she lives." Sienna taunted. "And how's your magic?"

"Let's find out." I snapped and threw a fireball at her.

She jumped sideways out of its path. I didn't wait for her to retaliate. Stone grew up around her, trapping her in a confined area. Fear and fury glowed in her eyes as she threw another fireball at me, followed by another. I easily twisted away from them.

"What happened to your clothes, pretty boy?" Sienna taunted.

"Some bitch thought I looked better without them." Kieran said and I couldn't help but smile at his response. Because she wasn't wrong.

Before I could mould magic in my hand, Sienna sent a flurry of fire rings toward us. Her hands turning black like molten and she released a snarl. My stone cage around her dropped as I dodged and weaved away from the fire rings. Jake and Clara threw yellow and green fireballs, but Sienna obliterated them before they grew near.

Sienna cackled, her hand facing Jake and Clara. I looked over my shoulder as a fire formed around them, trapping them in a dome. They dropped to the ground, covering their faces. *No, no, no.* I watched for a moment as they coughed and splattered in the smoke from the flames.

Tori glanced at them, but held her focus on the doorways. I spun around, catching Kieran's eye before he threw a frenzy of violet at Sienna. I shifted the stone around her feet, bringing pylons up. Each one created. She easily blasted into pebbles at the same time as holding a shield in front of her to counter Kieran's strikes.

I reached my hand toward Kieran, the other hand

outstretched toward Sienna. Kieran glanced at me for only a moment before replicating me and gripping onto my hand. Violet and turquoise glowed, electric fireballs entwined together. Sienna's eyes widened.

Releasing the magic, it hit Sienna square in the chest and blasted her backward. She hit the stone wall metres behind her, falling and crumpling at the base. A trickle of blood seeped through her hair. Her body was limp. I stepped forward and Kieran pulled on my hand.

"Wait." He said. "Are you sure she's…?"

I looked over my shoulder at her unmoving figure and the blood-soaked hair.

"Yes, I'm sure." I strode away from him, closing the space between Sienna and I.

Thud. Thud. Thud.

My heart pounded in my chest as I drew near. I wiped my palm on my pants. Taking a breath, I reached for Sienna. Her eyes flew open, and she grasped me by the throat. *Not again.*

"TRIXIE!" I heard Kieran yelling.

I gasped for the air my body begged me for — my lungs burned. My face turned purple from the lack of oxygen as I squirmed and hit at her arms to release me.

"TRIXIE! KIERAN!" Tori's voice cut through the pulse in my ears.

Why was she yelling out Kieran's name? Wait. *Where was Kieran?* Barely being able to see through my blurred vision, I searched for him. My eyes widened when I saw

Kieran suspended ten metres in the air.

Sienna was killing us both at the same time. Her hand outstretched toward him—fire wrapped around his body. *No. Not happening. She won't do this.* I closed my eyes, releasing all thoughts of my lungs burning and of my heart beating like it would burst.

The pressure around my throat released, and I gasped and coughed, opening my eyes wide. I spun to face Kieran. His feet dangled, his arms out wide. The fire spiralling around him vanished, and he fell.

I screamed. "KIERAN!"

Stone lifted from the ground, it whirled up, and wrapped around his body. It jolted his body, halting him from the free fall. Gradually, I brought him down to the ground safely. The stone melted back into the floor.

The fire dome dissolved, and the smoke released into the air. Tori bolted to Jake and Clara. Clara shook her head, waving her away. Tori gripped Jake and rolled him over. His chest rose and fell. Tori lent over and planted her lips to his. He held her close, my heart warming. *Finally.* I tore my eyes from them, back to Kieran. He lifted his head, his eyes locking on mine momentarily before staring past me.

Turning on my heel, I refocused on Sienna. I frowned as I stared at her trapped body. She was trapped with her arms moulded into the wall and her feet planted in the stone ground.

I glanced over at Tori, and she smirked at me. I

grinned back at her and brought my attention back to Sienna.

"Now...what to do with you?" I said, but I wasn't really asking her. "Well, the obvious thing would be best."

"Please, we're sisters." Sienna begged.

"Sisters?" I spat. "You never got that privilege."

Sienna's face crinkled, and she cried. "P-please."

"Oh, please." I rolled my eyes. "Did you really think I would believe those fake tears?"

Sienna pouted. "Worth a try."

I reached inside my jacket for Ivy, but she wasn't there. Sighing, I plucked Storm out of its sheath. I ran my fingers carefully along the blade and raised my eyes back to Sienna.

I stepped forward and pressed Storm against her forehead.

"My family has turned me into a killer." I mumbled. "But, they've deserved it."

Sienna trembled, her breathing thick as she kept her eyes on mine. There was no mercy for her.

I grazed the knife's edge along her face and down her jawline. Thin cuts pierced her skin, tiny drops of blood flowed down her face. I rested Storm's blade along her throat, pressing until blood appeared.

Sienna didn't dare swallow. Actual tears formed in her pleading eyes.

"Goodbye, sis-*ter*." I spat the last syllable.

I tightened my grip on Storm, ready to slice across her throat, but my eyes caught sight of her Soul Weaver's mark and I halted. Without it, we are nothing. I eyed Storm's sharp blade and glimpsed her mark.

"You know what?" I said, slowly moving the tip to the side of her neck.

Sienna's eyes widened.

"You deserve to live in suffering, with no parents, no siblings, and no magic."

"No, please—"

I pressed the blade into her flesh and carved the Soul Weavers mark off her skin as she screamed.

Twenty-Eight

WE STEPPED OUT OF THE swirling portal onto the glass platform in Myrdreya. Lightning flashed through the clouds, rain drizzled down, but the shield kept it from falling on us.

Suspended between Jake and Kieran was Levi. I couldn't leave his lifeless body back in the castle. He made mistakes, but he made up for them for everything he did for us. He became a part of our Soul Weaver family.

We strolled through the city — the beautiful crystal

glass had no shine. Soul Weavers we passed stared and whispered amongst themselves. I kept my eyes straight forward, avoiding the gazes I knew were on us all.

I had dreaded Kieran dying by the hands of my ex-family — not Levi. But it was the risk that we had all taken to save Kieran.

MORNING SUNLIGHT FILTERED down, penetrating through my closed eyelids. Soft fingers swirled on my back in a soothing motion. I smiled, opening my eyes and rolling over.

Kieran laid next to me, propped up on his elbow. My eyes wandered down his body, across his scarred chest, over the perfect v-shape leading to his groin. My breath caught — my girly bits tingling.

I scooted myself closer to him, placing my hand on the scarring on his chest. Everything he endured was because of my family. We both had endured so much from them. And now it was all over. They couldn't hurt us anymore. Although Sienna lived, she was sent back to the mundane world and left to live out her days magic-less. She did everything to get all this power, to only lose it all.

I leaned down and kissed all over his scar. His body tensed, but he didn't pull away. His free arm slipped under the sheet and around my waist, his hand resting at the small of my back. My lips grazed his skin, and I kissed my way up his neck to his scarred cheek.

He shuddered and tilted his face away from my lips.

"Don't hide from me." I whispered, my hand turning his face back toward me. "You are as handsome as the day I met you. Never forget that."

His Adam's apple bobbed, and his eyes searched my face.

"I'll have to start hiding my face if you hide yours." I said.

He groaned and nudged my nose with his. "Okay, deal."

I pressed my lips against his and wedged my tongue into his mouth. I twirled my tongue around his and sucked on his bottom lip. A soft moan escaped his throat. I smiled against him and pulled away.

"You can't tease me like that," Kieran groaned into my neck, "or we'll never leave this bed."

Giggling, I twisted away from him, sitting up. "I better stop then."

He groaned again, curling his body around me. "Aw, do we have to?"

I sighed. "Levi's funeral today."

Kieran pushed himself up and kissed my shoulder gently.

"Thank you." I mumbled.

"For what?" He asked, rotating his head to see my face.

"Organising a funeral for him." I looked over my shoulder at him.. "I really appreciate it."

"I know how much he meant to you."

My heart warmed, and I pecked him on the lips. "And that's why I love you so much. You're so caring and selfless."

⁂

AN HOUR LATER, Kieran and I were dressed in black leathers and strolling hand in hand to the south end of Myrdreya. He wore leather pants with a silver chain hooked at his left hip, and a black buttoned shirt. The dress I wore had a deep leather-bound plunge neckline, a bare back, and a flowy material down past my ankles. Kieran's hand moved to rest on my back as he steered me toward a sea of black.

A crowd all dressed in black leathers gathered along the edge of the city—the entire city was there. They parted, making a pathway for us to walk through.

Clara gave me a small smile as we passed. She had dyed her hair black and plaited it to the side, complimenting her long black leather and lace dress with thin straps. I smiled and indicated her attire with my free hand with a thumbs up.

She mouthed, "thank you."

On the other side of us stood Jake and Tori, their hands entwined. Jake wore black leather pants and a black t-shirt. Tori wore a cocktail dress with straps criss-crossing up the back. Her blonde hair sat neatly over one shoulder. My heart warmed at the sight of them—back together again.

Kieran led me to the front of the crowd. We turned and faced them. *Oh, god.* All eyes were on him—no, *us.* Of course, with Demetri gone, someone had to lead. It never occurred to me it would be Kieran.

"Thank you, everyone, for gathering here today." Kieran raised his voice to allow every Soul Weaver to hear. "I know most of you didn't have the privilege of knowing Levi. He was a selfless and caring human being. He put himself in front of danger and it cost him his life, saving our world from the destruction.

"Today, we put him to rest." Kieran turned to me. "Trixie, will you do the honours?"

I swallowed, my gaze sweeping over all the eyes now on me. "I would be honoured."

Kieran nodded to Clara, and she stepped toward me with a small black glass container I hadn't noticed her holding. She held it out to me.

"His ashes." She whispered and pointed to the edge of the floating city.

I nodded and took the container from her. I didn't know how I knew what I needed to do. I just knew. Walking toward the edge of the glass, I stopped half a metre from it.

Focusing on the glass edge, I breathed in deeply and

the glass moulded in a short pillar up toward me. It stopped at waist height and then formed a goblet on top. I unscrewed the glass lid and poured Levi's ashes into the goblet. Whispers in the crowd behind me reached my ears, but I focused on the task at hand.

"Thank you, Levi." I whispered. "You're free now."

I pushed on the glass with my mind. It extended away from me; the goblet sitting a metre out from the edge. Taking a breath, I released the warped glass. The ashes fell and floated away in the morning breeze.

A single tear fell from my eye. "Goodbye, Levi."

KIERAN CLASPED MY hand as we strolled through the garden and past the waterfall. Only scarring remained from his burns.

After all that had happened throughout my life, where I was now, I knew I belonged. Zalindor was truly my home now. Kieran was my everything, my soul bonded.

"Why was Sienna able to take your gift, but failed taking mine?" I frowned.

"You know, I was thinking about that earlier," Kieran said. "She had a stone in her hand when she siphoned me. Did she have one with you?"

I shook my head. "No. When she had locked up, she mentioned she needed something else, didn't say what.

The stone must have been the source of power to take gifts."

"Yes, I think you're right," he nodded. "She failed to take yours because she didn't have the stone, but I guess she tried anyway."

We passed the fountain, and I dipped my fingers into the cool water. Kieran gripped my hand and swung me around to face him. I placed my hand on his chest and looked up into his mesmerising brown eyes—I'll never get over those beautiful silver specks in his iris'. He tucked a strand of hair behind my ear and his fingers traced down my jawline.

"You will always be handsome to me." I said, running my fingertips over his scarred cheek. "Do you know why?"

He shook his head, his eyes studying my face.

My forefinger touched his bottom lip. "Because you saved me."

About the Author

Chantelle Lambert grew up on the Sunshine Coast, Queensland, Australia. She spent much of her childhood on the Sunshine Coast before moving to Brisbane for her high school years. When she was nineteen, she moved states to the Central Coast of New South Wales where she met her husband, Ryan Lambert.

They have a beautiful daughter together who inspired her to chase her dream as a writer.

Chantelle spent a lot of her time growing up writing short stories and going off into the imaginative world. She loves the magical fantasy world in particular. She has read so many fantasy books, which have been her inspiration over the years to keep writing and to follow her dreams.

Her passion for writing and history of anxiety and depression lead her to write this fantasy novel.

Connect with Chantelle online:

www.facebook.com/pg/chantellelambertauthor
www.chantellelambert.com.au

SOUL WEAVER DUOLOGY SEQUEL

Attacked in his own home, his port Kieran to safety and sacrifice themselves tot heir enemy. But, who was this enemy? Who took his parents' lives away from him?

Kieran learns to live in the Soul Weaver's city without anyone he knows, making friends while seeking revenge.

Will he succeed or does he lose more than just his parents in the process?